The Christmas Cracker
A Holiday Novella
Juliet Thomas

Clay Princess Publishing

Copyright © 2023 by Juliet Thomas

All rights reserved.

No portion of this book may be reproduced in any form without written permission from the publisher, Clay Princess Publishing, or the author, Juliet Thomas, except as permitted by US Copyright law.

No portion of this book may be included or used in the teaching and/or training of any form of AI nor may it be used for any purpose by AI.

This is a work of fiction. Names, characters, businesses, places, events, locales, and incidents are either the products of the author's imagination or used in a fictitious manner. Any resemblance in actual persons, living or dead, or actual events, is purely coincidental.

Although the author and publisher have made every effort to ensure that the information in this book was accurate at the time of press, the author and publisher do not assume, and hereby disclaim, any liability to any party for any loss, damage, or disruption caused by errors or omissions, whether such errors or omissions result from negligence, accident, or any other cause.

Cover design by Juliet Thomas

For the bestie who blessed me with her stream of consciousness one night:
This one's for you, KJ.
I hope I did it justice.

Contents

1. Tristan — 1
2. Charlie — 12
3. Tristan — 21
4. Charlie — 27
5. Tristan — 35
6. Charlie — 40
7. Tristan — 53
8. Charlie — 68
9. Tristan — 78
10. Charlie — 88
11. Tristan — 99

Grandma Jean's Thumbprint Cookies — 112
Battlefield Special Cocoa (Made at Home) — 115
Acknowledgements — 117
About the Author — 119

Chapter One
Tristan
December 11th

Buzz! Buzz! The annoying sound of my alarm rings loudly in my ears. Too loud. Smacking the small, black box on my nightstand, I pull the covers up over my head. I'm not ready for today. Knox roped me into showing up at the Christmas party tonight. I own half the security company; you would think I could skip just one event. Especially one my partner's wife planned. She's not my wife and they'll definitely be there. Besides, Lilian set me up with a blind date for the night. Not my kind of thing. *What was her name? Hell, I don't even care.*

As I slide the covers off my face, the picture I wake up to every morning comes into blurry view. My wife, well, ex-wife, and I on our honeymoon in Vegas. Christmas was Piper's favorite time of year, so it made sense that she wanted to get married on the day. Our wedding colors were red and green and there were twinkle lights and candy canes everywhere. You'd think the woman came straight from the North Pole.

We even checked something off her bucket list when we honeymooned in Vegas—Glittering Lights. Millions of Christmas lights and her eyes shined brighter than all of them. But that was years ago. She won't even look at me now. One day I'll stop torturing myself the moment I wake up and I'll toss that picture.

I climb out of bed and pad to the kitchen in search of coffee. Lots of coffee. *Maybe Irish coffee.* The cabinet above the coffee pot is where I stash the good stuff, but when I open the door, every coffee pod I've tossed in there comes tumbling out. Luckily, I catch the silver flask of whiskey before it falls too. No party fouls this early. Maybe I'll just stick with the Irish part. I unscrew the cap and take a swig, eyeing the pods strewn on my counter. Reluctantly, I pop a pod into the coffee maker and click it on.

After breakfast and a shower, I pour my coffee into a tumbler, grab my keys, and head out the door. The cold air cuts through me like a knife. I'd much rather be spending my Saturday night in bed like every other Saturday and not being forced to socialize, but here we are. I really should go pick up something to bring tonight. Though it's my company that's paying for everything. In a sense, I've already bought something for tonight. Honestly, if it wasn't for Knox and Lilian already telling this woman I'd be there, I wouldn't go at all. Christmas is great for everyone else; everyone else isn't haunted.

I spent the better part of the day processing paperwork. I've got two new classes of trainees coming in after the first of the year and clearing everyone for my program takes time. Sixty-two newbies, all gung-ho to learn from the SEALs. And I'm about to take a two-week vacation to the middle of nowhere. A secluded cabin up in the mountains, far away from any of the stressors here at work. No need for fake smiles and pretending to be happy. Spending Christmas alone with my misery sounds like Heaven.

A slap to my back makes me jump. "Ready to meet your next ex-wife tonight, T-Rex?" *Knox*. He sits down across from me at his desk and leans back, putting his hands behind his head.

"I'm ready to go to bed," I pause, leaning into the last word. "Alone."

"Come on, man. It's alright to let loose and have a little fun." He notes my unamused facial expression and adds, "Lilian's excited for you to meet Tara. Could you paste on a fake smile for Lil at least?"

I grunt and nod in agreement. Knox and I were on the same SEAL team. We departed at the same time but for different reasons. Lilian and Piper were as close as Knox and I are. But when Piper left, she left all of us in the dust, Lil included. Lil stuffed her sadness down around me. For her, it was like losing a sister. She and Knox got me through the worst of it. If I'm being honest, I would've drank myself to death if not for Lil. She made sure I ate, showered, and touched grass. I owed it to her to at least give tonight a try.

"Good." He moves to stand. "Welp, I'm heading to pick up the ol' ball and chain. I'll see you back here in an hour." He gives me a small punch to the shoulder and then heads out the double doors.

The party was in full swing when I arrived—half an hour late. Lilian spotted me first. She crossed the room and caught me by the arm, pulling me out to the hallway.

"So good of you to grace us with your presence. You know you've kept Tara waiting?" She leans in and sniffs the air between us. "Did you fall in the whiskey barrel or jump in of your own accord?" she asks, scrunching her nose at the odor.

I clear my throat, trying to speak softly to the small but mighty woman in front of me. "Liquid courage. I might've been a little nervous. Sorry I'm late."

"Nervous? Yeah, okay. That's a lie. And 'sorry I'm late'? This is your company, Tristan…"

"I'm sorry. I'm preoccupied. I'll make sure to apologize to your friend." She narrows her eyes at my words. "And I'll make it believable."

She nods her head and grabs me by the wrist then leads me to Knox and her friend, Tara James. By all accounts, Tara's pretty. Soft blue eyes, sandy blond hair, kind of on the tall side with legs for days. And her tight, dark green dress is short enough to show them off. To everyone. *I'd bet money she was a cheerleader in high school.* I hold my hand out to shake hers and she hesitates before she slips her soft hand in mine.

"Tara, this is Tristan Conrad, T-Rex, this is Tara James. You two talk; Knox and I will grab us some more drinks." She gives me a once over before adding, "Water for you."

Lil and Knox disappear into the crowd of our employees and their families, so I turn to Tara. "How long have you known Lil?"

She flashes a bright smile, scans me up and down, and pulls her bottom lip between her teeth. "We were sorority sisters at State. I was her little. Go Delta Zeta!" She shoots a closed fist into the air. *Ah. Definitely a cheerleader.*

"What did you major in?"

"Eh, it doesn't really matter. I didn't finish anyway. Partied my way right out of the sorority and school. I'm a dental assistant now." She gives her hair a flip. "So, tell me about you. You were in the military, like Knox?"

I give a stiff nod, "I was."

"Ooh, did you see any action? Have any cool stories? Scars? Oh! Do you still have your, uh, ya know, the clothes... the camo ones? Uniform! Do you still have your uniforms?" There goes her bottom lip disappearing between her teeth again. *How long does it take to get a few drinks?*

"Yes I did, depends on if you consider seeing your brothers die in front of you to be 'cool', a few, and yes."

Her eyes widen and part of me knows I've taken it too far. *I can't make it to the mountains fast enough. I'm really not this big of an asshole all the time. Gruff, yes. But not a total dick. God, I hate this time of year.* I clear my throat. "I'm sorry. It's been a long week."

She smiles again, "That's okay. It has been for me too. You'd be surprised how crazy it can get in the dentist's office." She finishes with a giggle. *Yeah, because it's definitely the same thing. Tristan, stop. She's a nice girl. This is just as awkward for her as it is for you.* "You kept your uniforms, huh? Do you ever... put them on for fun time?"

Thankfully, Lil and Knox make it back just as I open my mouth to say something I'll regret. "Everybody playing nice over here?" Knox asks, handing me a mug of coffee. Thankfully, he convinced Lil to let me have something stronger than water. Tara smiles again but gives Lilian some serious side eye and pulls her away, saying they're going to check out the food.

Knox nudges me with his elbow. "You okay? I know this isn't the best time to be set up on a blind date, but you know how Lil is. Once she gets something in her head... woman's a damn dog with a bone."

I chuckle. He's not wrong. "It's alright. I know she's trying to look out for me. She should know that her airhead sorority sister is probably not it though."

He laughs, "I tried to tell her. She needs better friends. But I bet you could take that one home with you tonight and never call her again and she'd be just fine."

I take a sip from the hot mug then say, "Yeah, as long as I put on my fatigues first."

"Seriously? Damn. I didn't know she was a uni chaser. Well, if you don't go after her, I bet Smoke would. She's just his type."

Funny, if you'd asked me 10 years ago, I would've told you Piper was my type. God, I loved that woman with every fiber of my being. It's the only reason I held on as long as I did. Maybe she was my type, and I just wasn't hers. Maybe I don't even know what my type is. I do know what it's not—Tara.

The girls walk back over to us, empty-handed, and the air feels a little different than it did before. The three of them engage in a conversation about the upcoming game of White Elephant that I'd forgotten about. No gift should mean that I can cut out of here when the game starts. The grating sound of Tara's giggle cements that idea.

Looking at all the guys with their wives and kids, I feel the familiar wave of grief begin to rear its ugly head. They say divorce is like dealing with the death of a loved one. The death of an entire life you'd planned out for yourself. I've been... dealing for the past two years, managing with the help of a Naval psychiatrist. I usually fight back the waves and don't let myself crash and burn, but I'm not sure that I can fight this one off. They say time makes it easier. I'll give them that I'm in a better state this year. Last year was my first Christmas without her in 10 years. I holed up in my apartment the whole month of December. Knox had to take over training new recruits while Lil made sure I was eating.

I relived every moment of it during the waking hours of that whole month. Getting the call that something had happened to her. Rushing to the scene. Knox trying, and failing, to stop me from getting to her. We'd had the worst fight of our entire marriage that night and she took off into a snowstorm. She'd turned around to come back home, hoping to make things work, when the idiot who decided a snowstorm was the best time for his second 30-pack slammed into the side of her car. She was out there because of me. She was coming back for me. It was my fault. Somehow.

Thank God she was okay, a shattered tibia, a broken femur, and some cracked ribs. But she was alive. Knox, Lil, and I waited hours at the hospital to hear any news. When she made it out of surgery, I went to her room to wait for them to bring her in. Thing was, I wasn't the only one waiting. Apparently, Piper had been seeing some little asshole on the side and since she was planning to leave, she'd changed her emergency contacts. They'd called him first.

Straightening my shoulders, I shake off the memories for the time being. A woman with such bright blonde hair it was almost white, wearing a gauzy, white dress walks up to the four of us with a basket on her arm. The basket is full of red and green colored foil-wrapped tubes. Christmas crackers. Another Piper favorite. She never wanted to share so she always made sure we popped our own. The woman hands each of us a cracker. "Don't forget to make your wish," she says, ice-blue eyes meeting mine as her hand lingers a little longer than it should. She moves on to the next group and I turn to Knox who's rolling his eyes. "They just flock to you, huh?" he says under his breath.

I shrug my shoulders, turning the cracker between my fingers. *What I wouldn't give for a do-over.* I'd take hold of the opportunities in front of me. Invest in something other than myself, my career. I twist the cracker until it pops, a small toy falling to the floor at my feet. I bend down to pick it up and turn it over in my palm. It's a tiny... rolling pin? Odd. Standing, I pull the small, purple paper hat from the tube. Small, thumbprint cookies holding chocolate kisses in their middles encircle the edges. This time, I have to admit it's kind of adorable.

"What'd ya wish for?" Tara asks, holding the contents of her cracker in a closed fist. "I wished for someone to give me a beach vacation for Christmas," she laughs.

"A do-over."

"Well, that's not very Christmas-y. You're supposed to make a wish about Christmas," she chides.

I shrug. "Won't come true anyway. I told you what it was."

"Hmm. I guess mine won't either. Dammit," her face falls and I'm pretty sure my negativity is starting to rub off.

Will, one of our main guys, stands on a chair at the head of the room and yells for everyone to quiet down. "Now that I have your attention. The most ruthless game of White Elephant can commence."

Time to exit stage left. Thankfully, the fact that I'm leaving town tomorrow proves a viable excuse. I say my goodbyes, making sure to tell Tara it was nice to meet her. And I don't decline when she gives me her number to call her later. Mostly because Lil is shooting daggers from her eyes and I'm honestly afraid of what that little firecracker is capable of. I shake Knox's hand and he pulls me into a half hug.

"I'll be back in two weeks. Hold down the fort while I'm gone?"

"I'll keep 'em in line," he replies.

Let's just hope the place is still standing when I get back.

Chapter Two
Charlie
Day 1

"*Are you sure you're going to be alright? All alone in the middle of nowhere. What if some mountain man breaks in? No one for miles, no one to hear you scream!*"

"Mom! Stop! I'll be fine! You and Dad enjoy your cruise. Mandy's more likely to get herself in trouble than I am," I say, trying to assure my mother. I've been looking forward to this for a month. There's nothing anyone can say that will keep me from spending two weeks, by myself, in the mountains.

"I heard that, Charlie!" my sister yells in the background. Mandy, my sister, was spending Christmas with her husband's family in Arizona while our parents had booked a 10-day Christmas cruise to the Cayman Islands. They hadn't bothered to clear it with us first, so I wasn't sure why Mom was so worried about it now. Did she think Big Foot was going to come snatch me up?

"Well, it's true. You're far more likely to find yourself in deep shit with your mother-in-law than I am to be kidnapped by Sasquatch."

"Charlotte Olivia Blaine! You watch your language," Mom shouts.

I sigh. My GPS speaks over my mom and my sister to tell me it's time to turn left. Just a few more miles up this mountain and I've reached my destination: silence and relaxation for a whole two weeks! This is the busiest time of year at the bakery. I even had to hire two extra people to deal with the influx of orders. But I might be a little too controlling given that they both quit on their third day. I always close up shop for Christmas, but this year I was taking a well-deserved vacation. Not that I wouldn't still be working. The bags and boxes of ingredients piled in the backseat of my small SUV were for the new recipes I planned to create while I was here. I wanted to start the year off with new things on the menu and what better time to experiment than during my time off? I did promise myself I'd put my plush, cozy robe and slippers to use tonight though. One night of pampering myself; watching a sweet Christmas movie with a fire going, all wrapped up warm and comfy on the couch, eating a big bowl of popcorn for dinner. It's going to be like Heaven.

"Sorry, mom. Okay, I'm not far. I'll send pictures to Mandy's phone when I get there. Love you both!"

"We love you!"

"Watch out for those mountain men!" my sister calls out, poking fun at our mom. I hear Mom call her by her full name this time before she hangs up. *Hah! It's not just me!*

A small, dimly lit log cabin sits nestled in a valley on my right. There are no other cabins anywhere around and the GPS tells me I've reached my destination before I can pull into the driveway. *I don't think the street is where I'll be sleeping, thank you very much.* The freshly fallen snow crunches under my tires and I wonder if I'll be able to get out of here tomorrow to get milk and eggs from the grocery store down the mountain. I grab my suitcase from the backseat and trudge through the snowdrifts to the front door. The owner I booked the rental with said there would be a hide-a-key somewhere near the front door, but the snow is so deep, I can barely get to the door itself. *At least it's not actively snowing now.* Digging in a drift, I find a plastic rock and flip it over. My fingers are so cold, I can barely open the door on the bottom. *Maybe if I hold my mouth just right...* Finally, the door pops open and I pluck the key from inside. *Yes!* I unlock the door and make my way inside.

In the corner of the living room sits a floor lamp that gives off the light I'd seen from the street. It's a lot bigger than it looked from the outside. The living room is open, spacious, with floor-to-ceiling windows on the back wall. The view of the mountains must be gorgeous in the daylight. I'm sort of mad at myself that it took me until late afternoon to get here and I missed the view on the first day. *Orders had to be filled. It's perfectly fine. I'll set an alarm to make sure I don't miss the sunrise.* To the right of the living room is a massive kitchen. *So much counterspace!* My heart leaps in my chest. *I cannot wait to get my hands dirty in here.*

The air inside the cabin was chilly, so I decided that before I allowed myself to get warm, I'd better unload my car. After I'd finished, I put my suitcase in the bedroom, lit a fire in both the living room and the bathroom—yep, one of those shared fireplaces for the bedroom/bathroom, *Heaven*—and put the contents of the ingredient boxes into the kitchen cabinets. Digging in the snow had chilled me to the bone. When I lit the fireplace in the bathroom, I noticed an amazing, large marble shower. *Well, I did say I was going to pamper myself.* Smiling to myself, I hurry to the bedroom to unpack my cozy robe and slippers. That's all I need to be comfortable.

The shower is even nicer than I realized. A huge showerhead hanging from the middle of the ceiling sends cascading water over my head like rain. I probably have the water too hot, but it feels like silk against my skin. I close my eyes and let the warmth sink into my muscles, my bones. Running my fingers through my hair, I make a mental list of what all I'd like to bake tomorrow. *Lemon blueberry crinkle cookies, cranberry mandarin orange muffins, blackberry cobbler...* My stomach growls. *Oops. Guess I should have more than popcorn for dinner tonight.*

Reaching for the bottle of shampoo, I pump some into my hand and work up a lather starting at the ends of my hair. *Did I remember to bring my hairbrush with me? It's so much easier to get the tangles out in the shower.* I feel around for it with my eyes still closed but it's nowhere to be found. "Must've left it on the counter," I say out loud. Carefully, I pry open one eye and step out of the shower. Sure enough, my brush is sitting next to the sink. As I grab it, I hear something thud in the living room. My heart races and I climb back into the shower. Another *thud.* I open my mouth to call out but nothing, not even a squeak. *This is it. Mom was right. Some crazed mountain man saw little alone me walk into this cabin and now I'm dead meat. A fish in a damn barrel.* Heavy footsteps move swiftly toward the bedroom, and I hold my breath. *Right, if I don't breathe, he can't see me. Real smart, Charlie.* I quickly grab the large bottle of shampoo and clutch it to my chest. *If nothing else, maybe I can hit him over the head and run away.*

"Hello?" a gruff, deep voice calls out from the doorway of the bedroom.

It's go time! Dammit, why didn't I take that Krav Maga class with Mandy??

The bathroom door swings open, and I fly out of the shower like a bat out of hell in all my naked glory. Swinging the shampoo bottle wildly, I miss every shot I take at the very tall, very wide, *extremely handsome* man standing in front of me with chestnut-colored hair and deep brown eyes as big as saucers.

"Ma'am!" he shouts, grabbing my wrists, effectively knocking the bottle out of my hands. He turns his head to the side as I try to wriggle free from his grip. He lowers his voice when he speaks this time, "I'm not going to hurt you! Just stop!"

"What are you doing here then!? Did you see me come in here?? Were you watching me the whole time, you perv!? I know *Krav Maga!* So... you better watch your back, buddy!"

"What? I just got here. I saw a car in the driveway, but I figured it was the guy I rented the place from. I didn't know anyone was here, let alone naked in the shower." His tone is more even now, if not a bit confusion-laced. "And if this is your idea of Krav Maga, I'd like to have a sit-down with the person who taught you how *not* to defend yourself."

I stand still as a statue. The cold air blows across my still-wet, and very naked, body causing a shiver to ripple through me. My cheeks flush hot with embarrassment. Quickly, I pull free and retreat to the safety of the running shower, slamming the door closed behind me. "Could you... step out for just a minute?" I ask timidly.

"Sure thing, tiny ninja."

The deep bass of his voice sends a different kind of shiver through me. *Shit. My clothes are in the bedroom!*

"Wait!" I yell, poking my head out of the shower door.

"Yes?" he asks, stepping back into the doorway, this time staring directly at the floor.

Cannot believe I'm doing this. "Would you mind grabbing my bathrobe from the bed and just tossing it on the floor there?" I point just outside the shower even though he doesn't look up. He grunts and stiffly nods, turning around to the bed then averting his eyes, partially closing the door, and hanging my robe on the hook.

"Floor's wet," he offers. "Wouldn't want to defeat the purpose." His eyes never leave the floor, and he turns to leave.

"Thank you," I finally call out to the already empty bedroom. *What just happened??*

I rinse the rest of the shampoo out of my hair and quickly climb out, toweling off and sliding into my robe. Wrapping myself tightly, I step into the living room to find the strange man kneeling in front of the fireplace, stoking a newly lit fire.

"I'm sorry I tried to attack you," I say, crossing my arms over my chest. He hesitates to look up at me, probably scarred from what happened when I pretended I was a spider monkey. A *naked* one, at that.

"All good," he says, standing to his feet. "Sorry I scared you."

"I think the person who owes us both an apology here is George. Apparently, he double-booked." I take two steps toward him and hold out my hand, "Charlotte Blaine. You can call me Charlie." His eyes move from my hand to my face and back again before he gently shakes it.

"Tristan. You can call me Tristan," he says gruffly. His attitude leaves a bit to be desired, but I gotta say, that jawline makes up for half of it. He shrugs off his coat revealing wide shoulders, bulging biceps, and from what I can tell, a chest carved from marble hides beneath the burgundy waffle weave shirt he wears. His faded haircut looks military, short tufts of brown hair stick up from the top of his head and a smattering of dark facial hair covers the bottom half of his face.

"Well, *Tristan*, this is quite the predicament we've found ourselves in." I run a hand through my wet hair creating a side part. "How long did you book the cabin for?"

"Two weeks. You?"

I chuckle, "Two weeks." *I really need this break. I need this cabin. But from how worn out the man standing in front of me looks, I'd bet money he needs it just as much. The situation isn't ideal but, life has handed me lemons before, and I always made lemon bars.* "Are you hungry?"

Chapter Three
Tristan
Night 1

I stare blankly at her. *Shouldn't we be figuring out which of us is abandoning ship? Not talking about dinner?* My stomach growls quietly. The liquid diet I chose for the day has left me on empty. "I could eat." A smile lights up her face. It stops me in my tracks. I can't exactly tell what color her hair is but considering how dark it is wet, I can't imagine it's much lighter than auburn. It's long, stopping at her waist, and wavy. *I'd bet it looks good pinned up.* The smile she's still wearing touches her hazel eyes that fight over whether they're green or gold. Her small frame seems smaller in my presence, and I'm having trouble forgetting what she looks like without the robe. *I tried my best to be respectful, really I did.* She's got a deep dimple in her right cheek that fades as her smile does. The next words out of her mouth yank me right back to the present.

"Oh, shoot! I forgot. I planned on going to the store in the morning for things like eggs and milk… and dinner things like meat."

I give her a half smile, holding up a finger, and cross into the kitchen. A large cooler sits on the floor by the refrigerator, and I open the lid. It's stuffed full of sandwich meat, steaks, chicken, ground beef, and pork chops—not to mention milk and eggs.

"Boy scout?" she asks, eyes wide as she starts to dig through the contents of the cooler. She opens the door to the refrigerator, kneels, and starts putting everything inside. *Guess she plans on leaving.*

"Navy SEAL."

She stops, looks up at me, and nods, saying with a smile, "Thank you for your service." Then she goes right back to emptying the cooler. No questions. No poking or prodding for more information. No stupid lines about wearing my uniform in the bedroom. Just her thanks. I pull out one of the bar stools at the kitchen counter and take a seat. When she finishes, she comes to stand across from me and leans onto her palms. "So, what'll it be?"

"You're taking this... too well. And this isn't a diner. I don't expect you to serve me. Or cook for me. Especially since you're leaving."

"Oh, I'm not going anywhere. And neither are you." The determination in her words catches me off guard. I'm never caught off guard. "At least not tonight."

"Wait, what?"

She smiles and that dimple makes a reappearance. "Tonight, we'll cook and eat dinner together. We'll stay nice and warm and *not* fall off the side of a mountain. The rest will be tomorrow's problem. We can puzzle this whole thing out then."

I eye her carefully, scanning her face and her... body... underneath that fluffy robe—watching her body language, of course. She's completely at ease. *Damn, she's sexy without even trying.* How she doesn't seem at all worried about sleeping in this cabin with a strange man she doesn't know is concerning. But I'm intrigued as to what she sees in me already to trust me this quickly. "What'd you have in mind?" The question comes off more suggestive than I mean and as the pretty pink flush creeps across her cheeks, I try to fix my fumble. "For dinner, I mean."

She stammers, "U-uh, d-dinner. Right. Um, well, I had intended to pop some popcorn and crack open a bottle of wine. Maybe watch a chick flick in front of a fire. But I would bet a man like you would need more than popcorn." Her throat bobs as she swallows, and all that confident easiness has melted away. Now she's the one eyeing me.

I chuckle, trying to ease the tension—though genuinely flattered that I've flustered her, even if by accident. "I do prefer meat and potatoes. There are some potatoes in that tote bag there by the cooler," I say, pointing to it on the floor. "And you put away plenty of meat." *There is not a way to keep that from sounding dirty.* "Steaks. I could cook steaks on the stove and potatoes could go in the microwave."

She scoffs, "No, sir. At least, not only in the microwave. Twice baked potatoes and some quick rolls. You cook the steaks; I'll handle the rest."

"And we ride at dawn," I joke. Thankfully, she lets out a small laugh, and the tension in her shoulders relaxes. She's right back to looking confident and wholly at ease. *I wish I'd had that effect on Piper.*

After dinner, I gathered our plates and cleaned up the mess we made while cooking. Somehow, the smell of Charlie's fresh bread had overpowered the smell of seared steak. The whole cabin still smelled like it was baking in the oven. Her twice-baked potatoes looked like tiny, white Christmas trees she decorated with herbs and spices. Dinner was phenomenal and it had nothing to do with my steaks; she'd made the sides the star of the show. I insisted on doing the dishes so that she could put her feet up and relax.

We were halfway into the bottle of red wine as I relaxed back onto the couch. She sighed contentedly and I hated that I was about to ruin her peace. "So, should we go ahead and talk about the plan for tomorrow? Just so we have an idea?"

She presses her lips together then pulls her wine glass to them and takes a small sip. "How do you feel about lemon bars?"

I stare at her, dumbfounded, then ask, "Lemon bars?"

"Yeah. I sell them in my shop on Mondays and Wednesdays. How do you feel about them?"

I shrug my shoulders. "I don't hate 'em."

"You know the saying about life giving you lemons? Well, see, when life hands me lemons—such as a double-booked cabin in the mountains—I tend to make lemon bars. Or lemon blueberry muffins. Oh, and lemon meringue," she pulls her bottom lip over her teeth on the last food item she mentions.

This woman is just rolling with the punches, no problem. Maybe it's my time as a SEAL or just my time in the military in general, but I'm a creature of habit. Going with the flow isn't my forte. "So, what I'm hearing is that you're about to make some lemon bars."

She laughs then takes a healthy swig of her wine before answering. "No. I could. But I don't plan on it tonight. What I'm saying is, I *need* this trip. And from the looks of those dark circles under your eyes, so do you. Do you want to murder me?"

"Not yet," I answer without thinking twice. Her face twists in shock. "Joking," I say, holding my hands up in surrender with a wide grin on my face. "You're safe with me, I promise."

She shifts, tucking her feet underneath her and shooting me a look like she might want to murder me now. "Don't forget..."

"You don't know Krav Maga? Yeah, you should really get your money back for that class."

Charlie laughs. When my expression doesn't change, she asks, "Are you serious?"

"Serious as a heart attack. Women should know how to defend themselves. Just in case. You never know when a strange man might walk in on you in the shower when you're home alone. Okay, maybe that was just this one time. Though there was that one movie..." She shifts in her seat. I can't fully tell if what I said made her uncomfortable or if she's now battling intrusive thoughts about me seeing her naked. Because I've been doing the latter since last night. *Time to change the subject.* "Anyway, If you were about to say that we're both staying for the duration, my only stipulation is that you let me teach you some ways to genuinely defend yourself while we're here."

A sly smile creeps across her pink, pouty lips. "Deal."

Maybe wishes do come true.

Chapter Four
Charlie
Day 2

Tristan did exactly what he said he would do and slept on the couch. He made sure the fire in the bedroom was out, and that I had plenty of blankets first, though. Still, when I woke up this morning, I was freezing. I wrapped myself in one of the blankets and stepped to the large window in the bedroom to find that half of it was covered in snow. A shiver ran down my spine at the sight. Snow wasn't exactly my favorite, but I didn't hate it either. And the peaceful sounds of the snow falling last night had lulled me right to sleep. Who knew we'd get this much.

Quietly, I tiptoe my way out of the bedroom, across the living room, and to the front door, carefully opening it. My attempt at being quiet was all for nothing when a large amount of snow topples inside the door at my bare feet, and I *yelp*. Tristan jumps off the couch at the speed of lightning, hair disheveled, knees bent, and hand on his hip. *Does he have a gun?* "It's just me!" I yell, holding my hands up. "I'm sorry!" His chest heaves with big breaths as the reality of what's just happened starts to fully set in.

"Shit, Charlie. Are you okay?" he asks, running a hand through the errant locks of brown hair on top of his head, the other still locked on his hip. He looks worried. Afraid. Small. Which is saying something considering the man's a damn giant. *6'4", if I had to guess.* Shutting the door and shoving most of the snow back outside where it belongs, I shake the icy wetness from my feet.

"I'm fine," I say. "Wet, cold, but fine. I'm sorry, I didn't realize half a snowman was going to fall inside the door." A shiver rolls down my body. My feet feel like icicles. Something clicks at his hip, and he removes his hand. "So, what is it that you do, Mr. Ex-SEAL?"

"Secret agent," he says, holding a finger to his lips. *Did he just make a joke?* He straightens fully and that look of fear is a distant memory. And I thought *I* had confidence. Though, I guess you would have to be pretty confident in yourself to have done what all he has. Not that I've asked, I didn't really want to pry into his past over our first meal hours after we'd met. But given what I know about the SEALs, I can imagine just fine without asking. He crosses the room and bends down to pick up something from the floor. The blanket. I hadn't even noticed I'd dropped it. He wraps it around me and guides me to sit on the couch.

Without a word, he kneels in front of me and picks up my feet, placing them on the tops of his thighs. With the bear paws he has for hands, he covers them both. The warmth from his hands is so intense on my frozen skin that it almost burns. The tingling and pricking in my toes intensify as he picks them up one at a time and *rubs my feet.* No man, let alone one who has known me for all of five minutes, has ever rubbed my feet. Tristan takes great care to use just enough pressure to keep it from tickling. He's not half bad at this. My leg relaxes on its own as he presses his thumbs into the arch of my foot. "You don't have to do that, you know," I say gently so as not to offend him; he's only being kind.

He nods his head, "I know I don't but thanks for the reminder. Getting warmer?"

Too warm. I shift my weight, heat creeping between my legs and spreading across my skin. "Yes, thank you. I can feel my toes again." He gives each foot a gentle squeeze and abruptly stands then digs something out of his suitcase in the corner. He kneels in front of me again, this time with a pair of wool socks, and slides them on my feet. *Okay, I'm confused. He went to sleep a big, scary bear and woke up a cuddly puppy. Minus the almost shooting me thing.* The roughness of his calloused hands against my calf sends goosebumps rippling up my leg. *Please don't notice.*

He pats my foot and swings both my legs up onto the couch. "How do you take your eggs?" he asks.

"In my waffles," I answer, scrunching my nose.

He lets out a small laugh as he tosses a couple of fresh logs into the fireplace. "Well, I can't say that my waffle-making skills would be up to your high standards. I gather that you cook professionally. Chef?"

I shake my head. The mystery, at least when it comes to me, is close to being over. And I'm starting to think he might really be a secret agent. Or maybe a detective.

"Baker?"

I touch the tip of my nose. "I own a bakery. I have a culinary arts degree, and I became a pastry chef after studying at Le Cordon Bleu in Paris."

He scoffs, "Well, Miss Fancy Pants, you can make breakfast then." Striking a match and lighting a bit of newspaper, he tucks it between the split logs. Then, he drops down onto the couch next to me. My entire body shifts from the force. "I take my waffles in threes." Tristan turns his head to face me with a glimmer of something mischievous in his eyes. "With chocolate chips," he adds.

There's nothing I can say. I've shown my hand. "Yes, sir."

"No need for the formalities."

Standing to my feet, I let the blanket drop. Instantly, I'm reminded why I wrapped myself up in the first place. The only things I'm wearing are a light pink silk cami and matching silk shorts. And Tristan's warm, wool socks. My feet are the only part of me saved from the icy chill in the cabin as the air hits my exposed skin. My nipples push against the silk fabric, hardening, growing more and more sensitive. The muscle in Tristan's jaw flexes. His eyes find the floor, and I do my best to not take it personally. *He's just being respectful. Even if it stings.* I cross my arms over my chest, covering the offending nipples for the moment, and head into the kitchen.

##

"Your waffles await your presence," I call out to Tristan who, while I made breakfast, only left the couch long enough to add more wood to the fire.

"You know, it's a good thing we managed to bring half a grocery store up here. That snow is deep. The weather report said to expect more as the day goes on," he says, sauntering over to the bar and taking a seat. I slide a plate with three chocolate chip waffles in front of him and place two strips of bacon, criss-crossed on top. He looks down at the stack of waffles then moves only his eyes up to meet mine. The hooded brown orbs peer into my soul, though I'm fairly certain he only means to send a silent request for more bacon. I place another strip on top, and he continues to stare. Slowly,

I drop one more on top and he lifts his head, smiles, and gives a firm nod.

"Pretty soon, we'll be buried in the stuff," I say as an involuntary shiver runs through me. Not sure if the snow is what caused it or the proximity to the man whose gaze could melt me faster than the sun will melt the mounds of frozen water outside.

Tristan takes a bite of the waffles and lets out a low moan. "My God, woman..." He stuffs a slice of bacon in behind it and *groans*. "How? It's just bacon. But it has--..." he finishes chewing then swallows before speaking again. "There's some kind of spice... cinnamon? Nutmeg? Something. What is that? Bacon is good, but the stuff I bought isn't *this* good."

Smiling, I answer, "Pinch of nutmeg, smidge of clove, dash of cinnamon. It's applewood smoked. Figured I would make it taste closer to an apple pie." He's halfway through the stack of pancakes and eyeing the plate of bacon that's left. "No, no. I will not be responsible for clogging your arteries or giving you a heart attack. I'm cutting you off." I'm only half-joking, but I slide the plate of bacon further away from him.

He pokes out his bottom lip and I sigh heavily, snapping a crispy slice of bacon in half and handing it to him across the counter. The smile on his face, the child-like joy, is heart-stopping. I turn my back to make my own plate; one waffle, two strips of bacon, and a handful of chocolate chips on top. By the time I spin back around to add the syrup, Tristan is taking his last bite. "Did you even chew!?"

He smirks, wiping his mouth with the back of his hand. "Once or twice. If you didn't make everything so good it melts in your mouth, maybe I would have taken more time. Take it as a compliment. You're not a terrible cook."

But was it really a compliment? "Thank you... I think," I say slowly. He gruffly nods, pushing the tight sleeves of his shirt halfway up his forearms. My eyes lock on the once-hidden tattoos. An eagle with wings spread wide carries a trident in one talon and a rifle in the other. An anchor sits in front of the trident and behind the rifle. Underneath the symbol, in bold lettering, One hyphenated word: T-REX. *Like the dinosaur?* The other arm brandishes a Latin phrase in typeset: *Non sibi sed patriae.* "What does that mean?" I point, asking without thinking twice before I speak.

"'Not self, but country,'" he answers, stiffening a bit. He doesn't delve any deeper. *Alright, military talk with a stranger is off-limits. I was right not to pry last night. I won't push today either.* I take two bites of my waffle before he stands to his feet, rounds the bar, and starts filling up one side of the sink with hot water and soap. When I give him a quizzical look, he answers my unasked question. "You cooked; I'll clean. Only seems fair."

"But you cleaned up last night, too. How is being on dish duty twice in a row fair?" *And who exactly are you? Where did the grumpy man who barely spoke last night run away to? Not that I'm complaining.*

"I'll make dinner tonight, and you can handle the cleanup. Since no one is leaving today with all that snow. Then we'll be even."

I raise an eyebrow. "You'll still be one ahead of me."

"Guess that means you'll have to eat a shitty omelet for breakfast in the morning. Whatever will you do?" he jokes.

Chapter Five
Tristan
Day 3

"Hold your hands up higher," I order. "How are you going to stop something from coming at your face if you keep your hands at your hips?" She drops her hands completely, letting them swing at her sides. I grab hold of her upper arms and squeeze tightly. "Do you remember what I showed you?" Determination mixed with indignation stares me in the face. Her eyes are a gorgeous shade of gold in the afternoon sun. Flecks of green sparkle around her pupils. I'm so lost in her gaze that I'm genuinely caught off guard when she lands a blow to the inside of my elbow, successfully freeing herself from my grip. "Shit! Good shot, Charlie." I rub the spot she hit. Not that it hurts but I want her to think it does. Confidence is key. Fear is what lands you in trouble.

She heaves a few breaths, the cold making it harder to take in air. We've been at this for hours. It was the first thing she wanted to do when she woke up this morning. Thankfully it hadn't dumped another half a foot of snow on us overnight but the sun wasn't melting this shit fast enough either. It's still a good 10 or more degrees below freezing out here. I know she's freezing and exhausted. There's plenty more I could teach her, but it doesn't have to happen all at once. It can't. Her chest rises and falls quickly and my eyes scan her body. The hoodie she's wearing can't possibly provide much warmth. The thin fabric hugs her curves tightly. She opted for yoga pants for "flexibility" but what she got was stiff muscles from the frigid temperatures. And I've been fighting off getting stiff myself, despite the cold. This was supposed to be a learning experience for Charlie, not an exercise in restraint for me.

"That's enough for today. Time to go in and get warm."

"Come on," she whines. "Just a little longer! I want you to teach me how to flip somebody."

"No way," I bark.

"It's all about leverage, right? Well, I'm little. I should be able to get the-..." She lunges at me, grabbing me by the wrist and spinning around, tossing my forearm onto her shoulder. "...-upper hand..." The words come out strangled as she tugs on my arm, trying with all she has to move me, even just an inch. My laughter from behind fuels her fire and I lose my footing for just a second. "Hah!" she yells, dropping my arm and turning to face me. "I did *something!*" I'm still shaking with laughter as she jumps in my arms and wraps herself around me. The laughter trails off but we're both all smiles.

"You did good, tiny ninja. Now let's get you warmed up." With her still in my arms, I walk toward the cabin.

Once we're inside, I drop her onto the couch and stoke the fire. Thankfully, it kept going while we were out there or the idea of getting warm would've been a pipe dream. She shivers, teeth chattering, and I fight the urge to warm her with my body heat. But, when I take off my jacket and sit down next to her, I lose the battle. Charlie crawls over to me, lifts my arm, and slides underneath it. She snuggles into my side and sighs.

"Dammit. I forgot the remote," she says, starting to lean forward. I pull her back and tight to my side. Reaching past her, I grab the remote from the coffee table then hand it to her.

"You're going to make me watch a cheesy Christmas movie, aren't you?" I ask, with as much fake disdain as I can muster. Truthfully, the corny Christmas romance movies where the girl and the guy fight against some sort of random, off-the-wall conflict to wind up together in the end? I love them. A cute little Happily Ever After. It was the one thing about Christmas that Piper wasn't fond of. She thought they were overdone and overplayed. I like the routine; knowing what to expect before it happens. It's comforting. And given the current state of Charlie's face, she feels the same way I do.

"We don't have to," she finally says, sounding like she might cry.

Taking the remote back from her, I turn on the TV in search of the channel that seems to play Christmas movies all year long. Charlie squeals just a bit when I land on it. A blonde-haired woman stands in front of a partially decorated Christmas tree while her male counterpart watches her stretch to place the star on top. Charlie settles back in, wrapping my arm tighter around her. I look around the room, only now realizing there's not a Christmas tree up anywhere. *Guess George isn't one for decorating.* I make a couple of mental notes then pull a blanket from the back of the couch and drape it over Charlie. She lets out a contented sigh.

It's dark out now that our movie marathon is over. I don't know about Charlie but my stomach is trying to eat my backbone. *Whose turn is it to cook? What I wouldn't give to just order pizza. Pepperoni, sausage, olives, pineapple, and jalapenos. Shredded pepperoni, though, because... it's just better. Less grease. Damn, I'm hungry.*

"Your turn or mine?" I ask, forgetting that she can't hear my thoughts or feel the gnawing pain growing in my belly.

"To do what?" Her eyebrows knit together when she looks in my direction.

I shift my body to face her fully. "Cook dinner. You ate my shitty omelet and did the cleanup this morning but you cooked last night too. Ya know what, never mind. I worked it out myself. Wait here." I move faster than expected and she slumps over onto the couch.

While I start opening cans and dumping things into a pot, she watches my every move. She just might be disgusted by my choices for the concoction she's about to eat. I'm positive she's critiquing my cooking skills. My technique may be less than stellar, but no one has complained about my food in the past. Okay, well, no one has died. Yet. *Shit, maybe I should've let her cook after all.* I will say, her facial expressions throughout have been... amusing. When the show's over, I start spooning goulash into bowls and she smiles at me. A beautiful, wide smile I'd chase to the ends of the Earth.

I've never been much of a believer in fate or coincidence. I think you get what you give and most of what happens in life is just pure, dumb luck. Wishes only come true in fairy tales. But, no matter what it was that brought us both here, I thank every part of the universe and God himself for sticking us in the middle of nowhere. It's only the third night, and I can already feel this broken heart being stitched back together.

Chapter Six
Charlie
Day 7

Thunk!...Thunk!...Thunk! The loud noise pulls me from what was a *great* night of sleep. Such an amazing dream about... Tristan. *Damn.* We stayed up half of last night, talking about everything from favorite pizza toppings to past relationships–he's divorced while I've been married to my job for the last 14 years. His favorite pizza toppings give you heartburn just listening to him rattle them off. And when he smiles, genuinely smiles, his eyes glisten in a way that could melt the coldest of hearts. His whole body relaxes. We popped popcorn and watched another Christmas movie. Well, *he* watched the movie. I fell asleep halfway through. I think he might like those cheesy movies more than I do. And then the dream came crashing like a tidal wave. A big, strong, sexy, tidal wave that engulfed all of my senses. Vivid dreams of his bulging biceps holding himself above me in the bed while a fire roars in the fireplace. I could hear his groans, smell the clean scent of his freshly showered skin, feel the scruff of his unshaven face, but most of all, I could taste his kiss. *Was it a dream?*

I sit up on the couch, shifting the blankets off my body and wondering if I slept alone last night or not. *Thunk!...Thunk!* Searching around the room, still partially asleep, I look for the source of the noise. Nothing. And no Tristan. His coat catches my eye, hanging on the hook by the door where he'd left it after bringing in more firewood yesterday afternoon. My foggy brain finally clears enough to put it all together: the sounds are coming from outside, Tristan is outside, and he isn't wearing a coat.

Quickly, I pad to the door, wrapping myself tightly in the blankets before grabbing his coat, stuffing my feet into my boots, and heading outside. I follow the deep-set footprints he left behind around the back of the cabin to an area filled with evergreen trees. *THUNK!* The sound gets louder as I get closer. Then I spot him, chopping down a beautiful, tall, and full fir tree, the branches heavy with fresh snow. He hits the base of the trunk once more and the tree starts to fall away from him. He swiftly grabs it just before it can touch the ground.

He has to be freezing. The waffle weave shirt he seems to love so dearly isn't warm enough for these sub-zero temperatures in the early morning hours. *His closet must be full of those shirts. Nothing but waffle weave everywhere, in an array of colors.* It was so cold, my teeth started chattering the moment I opened the door. But, damn if this sight wasn't worth freezing my ass off to see. The man looks like a whole lumber*snack*!

"You left something inside," I say when I get about five feet away.

"Don't need it," he grumbles.

Okay, Mr. Grouchypants. "Come on, you're going to catch pneumonia being out here with no coat. Put it on. It's freezing." I take another couple of steps toward him and hold the coat out for him to take.

Tristan turns and as the sunlight reflects off the snow, his eyes look like honey. Raw honey. A deep golden brown. He gives me a quick once over. "You're wearing next to nothing, of course you're freezing."

"Take the damn coat, put it on, and then you can continue letting out your aggression on the trees. Not sure why you're cutting more firewood anyway. There's a stack that comes up to my boobs inside."

He chuckles, taking the coat from me and sliding it onto one arm while the other props the tree up. "This isn't for burning," he says, shrugging on his coat the rest of the way. The confused look on my face must tell him that I need an explanation because he follows up with, "It's a surprise. You'll see. And I'm not aggressive. Just had a job to finish."

My teeth chatter and I pull the blankets tighter around me, hoping they'll somehow be able to block out the chill from the wind.

"Go inside and get warm. I got a fire going this morning before I came out here."

"Nope," I say, stomping once and effectively knocking a whole boot full of snow in and around my foot." Shit, that's cold. But solidarity, sir! I'll go in when you do." I give him my cheesiest fake grin.

He looks me directly in the eyes and pleads, "Please stop calling me that."

"Yes, si-... I mean, sure. Sorry." *Uh-oh. I guess we're living in Grouchland today. Bad dream? Oh God, did I snore? Did I talk in my sleep!? Did I say something offensive? The only offensive thing about my own dream was that it ended.*

Tristan adjusts his hold on the tree and lifts it off the ground. His face softens with his next words, "No, *I'm* sorry. Had a tough time sleeping this morning. And I know you don't mean anything by it, but I'm just–" he stops, seemingly searching for the right words. "I'm not your superior. I'm not above you."

"I beg to differ," I start, looking up at him and waving my hand around in the foot plus height difference between his face and mine. "You're absolutely above me, ya giant." I watch his face for any hint of humor and when I see a small smirk, I pounce. "For that matter, you also have bigger muscles. *Plus!* You cook better steaks than I do. So, superior."

His smirk grows into a full-on smile that brings laughter with it. I don't need a fake grin this time, his smile is contagious. Giving a nod in the direction of the cabin he says, "Inside, Charlie." I pull the blankets tighter again, needing them less now that Tristan isn't throwing ice my way, and we head back inside.

One of those plastic, deep green bases you put a real Christmas tree into is set up in the empty corner of the living room to the left of the fireplace. *Has that been there the whole time?* Tristan sets the tree down into it then kneels to tighten the screws at the bottom so that it stands up straight and tall. The thing is slightly taller than he is but there's still room between the tree and the ceiling for whatever we put on top.

"It's sacrilegious or something to not have a Christmas tree up. I thought maybe... well, I found a few strings of lights in the closet this morning," he says, crossing the room to a linen closet set into the far wall.. "No ornaments though."

"That's okay! I can make salt dough. We'll just make our own ornaments. Oh, and we can string up popcorn and the cranberries I brought for orange cranberry walnut muffins."

His face twists a bit, "Yep. I'd much rather those go on the tree if that mouthful of a muffin is what you'd intended them for."

"Hey, I ate your shitty omelet and didn't complain. You could *try* an orange cranberry walnut muffin. You might find out you like it," I snap back in a joking tone.

"I knew it!" he exclaims. "Knew you thought my omelet was beneath you."

"I'd like to be beneath you." *Nope, no, said that out loud. Shit.*

Tristan clears his throat. I'm really trying not to take offense but the rejection is starting to do a little more than sting. It would be different if this was day one; or even day three. But it's the end of the first week. We've spent every waking, and last night even sleeping, hour with each other. The chemistry is there. I feel it. I know he has to feel it too. Hell, he's seen me naked. *What if that's the problem? He's seen it all and he doesn't like it? Ouch. Okay, we went from stinging to full-on hurt.*

I take the lights from him and set to work untangling them on the couch in silence. He paces the floor for a minute then disappears behind me into the kitchen. It takes everything I've got to not turn around and see what all the noise is as he clangs pots and searches the refrigerator and cabinets. But I'm still licking my wounds and pretending that I don't care.

A few minutes later, I've untangled the three strings of lights and Tristan comes back with a mug full of light brown liquid. A candy cane pokes its crook out from the top and marshmallows float on the surface. *Hot cocoa. My favorite thing about Christmas.* "Thank you," I say, not looking at him when I take the hot chocolatey goodness from him.

"Battlefield special," he offers. "I spent a few Christmases out on ops and a team member, my second, always threw this together. A little taste of home." I note the tiny bit of information spillage. My eyes meet his and I realize this cocoa is his apology. *Is the tree an apology? For what? Can I ask? Ready or not...*

"Besides the fact that it is all sorts of wrong to not have a Christmas tree, what made you jump up this morning to chop one down?"

He takes a deep drink from his mug then runs the tip of his tongue over his top lip before answering. "My therapist says I should talk more openly about these things. But," he places his mug on the coffee table, taking a string of lights from me as he continues. "It feels like weakness. She calls bottling it inside the weak part. Not willing to be in control of my own shit. I get it, but if it fucks with me, wouldn't it be worse to put that on someone else? Let it fuck with them too? Seems wrong. Although, the way I've done it for years hasn't been very effective. So, I'm trying a new approach," he finishes, wrapping the last of the first string around the tree then holding out his hand for another.

"Chopping down trees?" I ask, half-kidding.

He smiles and begins wrapping the second string of lights around the tree. "Not exactly. Usually when I… well, we'll call it 'struggle with sleeping,' I spend the rest of the day in my head. I keep to myself, I torture myself with the same images and thoughts and remind myself that it's my fault. And then I'm an asshole. I lash out at anyone around me. The therapist says to get active. Well, there's not a heavy bag here. I don't really want to punch a tree or get frostbite trying to jog in two feet of snow. Kind of prefer my hands unbroken and having all my fingers and toes. She says not to let it stew; to write it down or say it out loud. Because it's going to come out one way or another. I'm in control of the '*how*' if I'm the one who says the first word." He takes the last strand and kneels in front of the tree.

I sip my cocoa. This is the first time he's been this open. When he told me he was divorced, he glossed right over it. It was, "I was married, shit happened, now I'm not. Been divorced for two years," and that was it. Not what happened, nothing about what added a steel coat to the Great Wall of China the man had built around himself–not another word.

So this, this is different. And he gets my full attention. I can't help but to try lightening the mood, "Obviously the tree didn't get the *last* word." He stops what he's doing and turns to look at me with a wide grin on his face.

"My therapist would call that classic avoidance, ma'am. I'll see your humor and raise you that I *always* get the last word," he says with a sly smile. I nearly spit out my cocoa. "Really though, I'm a work in progress and this tree is part of that. You've noticed every tree in each Christmas movie we've watched. You point out what's on them, the multicolor lights vs the white lights, even what type of tree they are, and the list goes on. So, instead of holding everything in, I chopped down a tree. Instead of lashing out at you later for something that isn't your fault, I gave you a symbol of Christmas that you were missing. Progress." He turns to look up at me again and asks, "Ready?" I nod, smiling so hard it hurts my cheeks.

He plugs in the tree and every one of the thick branches sparkles to life with brightly colored lights. It's *gorgeous*. Red, green, blue, pink, and yellow pinpoints of light begin to blink as they warm up. He stands to his feet, stepping back to take a look, then wraps an arm around my waist. I don't move, afraid I'll spook him and the last thing I want is for this moment to end. Tristan looks down at me, his eyes warm, a soft smile on barely parted lips and I am absolutely certain he's about to kiss me.

Suddenly it's like I've fallen into a snow drift. His expression hardens again and he moves away from me, the absence of his warm arm leaving me chilled to the bone. I don't think I've ever met a more frustrating man in my life. I take a deep breath and do my best to shake it off, plastering a smile on my face. I am happy that he got me a Christmas tree, regardless of the reason it happened. But now it needs ornaments. And I need something to keep me distracted.

Crossing to the kitchen, I pull a large metal bowl from the cabinet and gather my ingredients for salt dough; flour, salt, and water. Simple, easy, mindless. I could do this with my hands tied behind my back. Tristan watches from the living room, looking uneasy. I wonder how well I'm hiding my hurt feelings. I add two cups of flour to the bowl, then a cup of salt, and lastly, a cup of water. Finally, I start to stir. When a nice ball of dough begins to form, it's too difficult to use the wooden spoon, so I sprinkle some flour on the counter and dig in with my hands. Once everything has come together, I dump the contents of the bowl out onto the counter and start kneading. Tristan is still watching my every move.

Did I make him this uncomfortable watching while he cooked? No, he smiled. He was probably laughing on the inside. I know my face was loud the first time. I've never seen anyone cook with such reckless abandon and it still turn out... edible. Who am I kidding, he could open a steakhouse. Does it even matter what happens before it gets on the plate? I laugh to myself at the last thought.

"What?" he asks, picking up his cocoa and taking a drink as he comes into the kitchen to sit.

"Nothing. Have you ever thought about leaving the security business behind and opening a restaurant?"

"Okay, that doesn't sound like nothing. What's going through that pretty head of yours?" he asks as casually as can be.

Full stop. Sir. You cannot with this emotional roller coaster. Did you have some sort of telepathic conversation with your therapist before you walked in here? Are we just forgetting the ice bath your actions gave me a few minutes ago?

"Just wondering, really. Your steaks were mouth-watering and while your technique might be unorthodox, you know how to deliver. I think it's your turn to cook dinner tonight," I say with a forced smile.

"I thought you were about to hit me with one of those compliment/insult combos. Something like, 'You can cook a mean steak, but you've got a face only a mother could love.'"

I slam the dough onto the counter harder than I mean to and try to play it off as normal kneading procedure, leaning into it further. *I could love your face, and I'm not a mother. At this rate, I never will be. At least I have buns in the oven when I'm at work. Married to my bakery for all eternity. Of course I can't get a man like him to give me a chance.* Tristan rounds the corner to my side of the bar when I've been silent too long.

"Can I help?" he asks. "I've never made my own ornaments before. At least, not ones that weren't cut out of construction paper when I was in grade school."

I need space. Just for a minute. I need him to not be this close to me.

"You know what? This is going to take a little while. Why don't you go grab a shower and I'll get these in the oven. By the time you're finished, they'll be ready and you can help me decorate them," I say, trying to keep my voice as even as possible. I don't want him to think I'm mad at him. Really, I'm not. I'm hurt, not angry.

Dejected, he puts space between us. "Oh. Uh, okay. I probably stink anyway. The whole chopping down... a tree... thing." He turns on his heel and rubs the back of his neck as he walks into the bedroom.

Dammit. I look like an idiot. A desperate idiot. Is there anything worse? If so, that's it. I'm that. Sure, let's just keep throwing yourself at the man who is obviously less than interested. Never mind the fact that he just almost kissed you. Okay, he didn't make it that far, but it definitely looked like it was coming. And then we took a hard left to Avoidance

City. Self-doubt, party of one. Your table is ready. Oh my God, we still have a week left. Keep your legs closed, Charlie, your hands to yourself, and your mind on... anything but him.

Chapter Seven
Tristan
Day 7

What did I say? Or not say? Did I do something wrong? Steam from the hot water of the shower begins to fill the bathroom. I tug my shirt up over my head and stare at myself in the mirror for a moment. The left side of my chest holds a sizable, ugly, red scar where there once had been a tattoo. I trail my fingers over the patch of uneven skin. It's the reason I don't walk around shirtless; why I've slept fully clothed every night here. It's unsightly. And it'll make Charlie ask questions. Questions I don't know that I'll ever be ready to answer.

For the second time today, memories flood my mind of my team out on an op, a rescue mission. We were tasked with bringing home a foreign dignitary. We made it, but not without incident. Our intelligence was wrong. An entire unit of soldiers from the opposition were lying in wait to ambush us. They tossed Molotovs at the building where they'd been holding their hostage. Flames licked at our skin as we searched, found him, and tried our damndest to get back out. I almost lost my entire team. Brought this scar home for my trouble and my brother, my second, home in a casket.

The fog on the mirror matches the fog in my brain as I try to pull myself back to the present. Blurry-eyed, I step into the shower and let the hot water stream over my head. If only it were as easy to wash away memories as it is to wash away the sweat of your day. Part of why Piper and I couldn't work is this right here. I play everything so close to the vest, holding in parts of me that have shaped who I am and how I feel. I don't want to make that same mistake. Not with Charlie. Her cheery disposition changes every time I...

Shit. Is that it? Does she think I don't want her? Of course she does. I give her every reason to think that way. Every time she tosses a suggestive comment my way, I say something to shut her down, shut her out, or I don't say anything at all. She's caught me staring at her more than once or twice. Boy, I'm an idiot. There's a beautiful woman in that kitchen right now who took a chance on a stranger. I made a wish then got plunked in the middle of nowhere for two weeks with someone I could be happy with if I'd let myself.

I cut the water off then step out of the shower, wrapping a towel around my waist. Water drips from my hair as I make my way out of the bathroom and into the kitchen like I'm on an op. Charlie's standing at the counter, cutting shapes in the dough with a steak knife and placing them on a pan. *This is it. Take the shot. As soon as she puts down that knife...*

She lays the knife on the counter and I take two wide steps to close the distance. Grabbing her by the waist, I turn her to face me. White streaks of flour stain her cheeks and her eyes are a rich golden color in this light. I don't take more than a second to drink her in before my lips crash into hers. They're as soft as I'd imagined them to be; soft like velvet. Charlie parts her lips and the moment her tongue meets mine, I can taste the peppermint from the cocoa I made. And somehow, even though I know she hasn't added spices to anything, she smells like cinnamon. *God, I could live or die right here in her kiss and either way be happy.* I cup her face in my hands and pull back to break the kiss. Her eyes are still closed, her breath coming out in short pants against my lips. Gliding my thumb across her swollen bottom lip, she damn near whimpers.

"Took you long enough," she says, the corner of her mouth tugging up into a smile. Her honeyed eyes open, hazy with want, need.

"Too long. I'm sorry," I breathe.

She leans back a bit, just enough to get a look at me. Her eyes train on the scar on my chest. She doesn't say a word as she runs her fingers over it. Leaning in, she plants a few light kisses to the rippled skin. Her eyes meet mine again and I press a kiss to her forehead. *I need her. I need her out of these clothes. I need her underneath me.*

"Bedroom?" she asks.

"Oh yeah," I say, wrapping my hands around the backs of her thighs and lifting her into my arms. She wraps her legs around my waist and covers my neck in kisses and gentle bites the whole way to the bedroom.

With Charlie wrapped around my body, I kneel on the bed. She catches my lips in a hungry kiss before I gently lay her down. I slide my hand underneath her loose, navy-blue tee and up to palm her breast. A lacy piece of fabric stops me from feeling the soft skin beneath. She pushes against my shoulders, moving me back a bit, and grabs the bottom of her shirt, wiggling as she lifts it up and over her head. My eyes scan her nearly naked body beneath me. Black lace meets porcelain skin in a display of beauty that would make the angels cry. I lean down and trail kisses from the hollow of her neck, along the edge of the black lace cup, to the valley between the two peaks. Goosebumps rise on her skin as my lips graze just underneath the edge of her bra. She groans, slipping a hand behind herself to unhook the offending fabric, tearing it off in a huff.

She's fucking beautiful. I want to take all the time in the world, savor every bit of her. *I need to see the rest.* Watching her face to make sure I'm not overstepping, I hook two fingers in the top of her yoga pants. She nods once and I tug them to her ankles in a flash. Matching black lace underwear stares back at me and... *God, my cock aches.* Freeing Charlie's feet from her pants, I toss them to the floor then remove the towel from around my hips and set my dick free. Hard and heavy, it stands at attention. Her eyes go wide. Not long ago, she saw me without a shirt for the first time and now, she's seen it all.

Slowly, keeping a close eye on my face, she reaches for my cock and grips the base, drawing me closer to her as she begins to stroke. I let out a half-moan, half-growl at her touch. Without thinking twice, I push aside her panties and plunge a finger inside her, curling it upward. The hot, wet, tight space mixed with the heady feeling of her soft hands sliding up and down my length, mirroring each other's motion, has me ready to explode.

Just then, three ear-piercing beeps sound from the kitchen. Then another round, and another. *Smoke alarm.* I withdraw my finger, jump from the bed, and race to the kitchen, unsure of what I might find. Rounding the corner, I see a fairly steady stream of dark grey smoke coming from the oven door. I wave one hand in an attempt to clear some of it from the air as I shut off the oven with my other. My first instinct is to open windows and doors, to vent out the smoke faster but as I look down at myself, I remember that I'm still *fully naked*. My naked ass took off running into this kitchen, hard as steel cock and all, just out for anyone to see. It's a good thing we're in the middle of fucking nowhere. I reach above my head and press the button on the smoke detector to make the incessant loud noise stop just as Charlie rounds the corner into the kitchen.

"Wildly unfair," I say, standing in front of the oven in all my naked glory while she's taken the time to at least put her shirt back on.

"Whatever do you mean, sir?" A playful smile dances on her lips.

Covering my shame, I cross to the front door and open it. The rush of frozen air takes with it any remnants of arousal that were left. Charlie removes the pan of burnt ornaments from the oven and sets them on top of the stove with a clatter.

"I'm taking my balls and going home. To the bedroom. To get some damn pants," I say as I walk through the kitchen.

She pulls the oven mitt from her hand and tosses it onto the counter. With a slight tilt of her head–pretty sure she's checking out my bare ass–and a hand on her hip, she asks, "Not taking the bat with you too?"

I glare at her over my shoulder. Charlie's hand shoots up to cover her mouth, stifling the full-on laughter to just a snicker. With a huff of breath, I take my leave.

It doesn't take long to throw on some light grey sweatpants. When I come back into the kitchen, Charlie's shutting the front door. It'll take the cabin a bit to warm back up but it's hard to notice the difference when my view is a smoking hot woman in nothing but a tee that hits midway over her ass cheeks, revealing a hint of those black lace cheeky underwear. All the blood rushes back to the wrong head. *Down, boy. Could use that ice-cold air right about now. Football, baseball... tight pants... wait a minute... no, like those tight yoga pants she practically lives in. My God, the woman is sexy in any state of dress.* I adjust myself but still turn to face the counter as Charlie comes back to begin placing more ornaments on a second metal pan.

She looks unhappy as she pokes at the flattened dough that's now cracked and brittle. "Kind of dried out while..." she trails off. Her cheeks blush a rosy pink. *Is she embarrassed? Nervous? The counter must be incredibly interesting given the hole she's staring into it.*

"Are you planning to ignore this?" I ask, jumping in with both feet to break the deafening silence. "Because I'm not. I know I've kept my distance and shrugged things off, but there's no denying the heat between us, Charlie. And there's no going back from what just happened in there," I finish, aiming a thumb over my shoulder at the bedroom.

Brilliant hazel eyes stare up at me as she chews on her bottom lip. She looks uncertain but given how wet she was for me, and most likely still is, I'm not sure what there is to be uncertain about. She takes a deep breath and says, "What if it's only because we're stuck here? Just us, you and me, in this tiny little cabin and you do these things like make me cocoa and bring me a Christmas tree... What if it's some kind of illusion that we'll lose the moment we walk out that door the day after Christmas? What if this is all we get?"

I chuckle, "Uh oh, you sound as cynical as me." She smiles at that. Tenderly, I wrap my fingers around her wrist and pull her body to mine, cupping her face with my hand, my thumb brushing her cheek. I press a gentle kiss to her lips then look her in the eyes and say, "Neither of us know what's going to happen when we leave here. We can't see what comes next. Does that mean we don't get to enjoy the moment?" I take a beat. "Damn. You're rubbing off on me."

"Well, I was trying to, but..." she starts.

The tips of her fingers find their way down from my hip to my now fully hardened cock. Remembering the way she feels, her warmth, the slickness of her excitement, has my balls tight in anticipation of release. I need her. I want her. And as I slide my hand between her legs, I can feel she wants me too.

There's no time to waste going back to the bedroom. I hook my thumbs at the top of my pants and in a flash, they hit the floor. Her tongue grazes her bottom lip, taking in the sight of me as she wriggles out of the black lace underwear. Gripping her hips I lift her onto the counter, desire to see and taste her taking over. Before I can satiate my hunger, she puts her hands on my chest and yells, "Wait!" Quickly, she hops off the counter, spins the knob on the oven, effectively turning it off, and looks up at me apologetically.

"Just making sure this time."

I stifle a laugh, lifting her back up onto the counter where I'll have the best access. She whimpers when I push her legs apart and my cock twitches at the sound. I don't hesitate to dive in, feasting on her as if she were the finest of dining experiences. She fists my hair, rocking her hips to the motions of my tongue as I lick, suck, and nip at her most sensitive spot. The breathy moans escaping her lips lead me on to the edge of her orgasm. I plunge my tongue inside her, desperate to taste her as she clenches, tightens, pulses, then lets go. She groans as she rides the wave of pleasure, spilling herself onto my tongue. I lap up every bit of it, her sweetness overwhelming my senses.

Swollen, still shaking, and hungry for more, she tugs my head up to press her lips against mine. Our tongues dance and she moans into my mouth as she tastes herself on me.

"Tristan," she whispers between furious kisses. "Please," she begs.

Panting, my cock throbbing, I ask, "Please what?" My words come out thick, dripping with desire.

"Please let me feel you." Her hands glide along my length and she moves to position herself on the edge of the counter. I cup her face with one hand and slip the head of my cock just inside her entrance with the other. Another whimper from Charlie as I tease circles and light brushes around and across her clit. She grabs my hip and almost jumps off the counter to impale herself on my cock. Our groans mingle in the still air of the kitchen as I glide in and out of her. *God, she feels amazing. So tight, so wet. Deeper...I need to feel all of her.*

I wrap an arm around her, pull her to my chest, and slip out of her. I turn her to face the counter and she bends at the waist, giving me a full view of the ass she hides in those yoga pants. My hand slides down and around the curve of her ass cheek as I squeeze and lazily let go.

"Mmm, may I?" I ask, needing her permission before...

She pushes herself back against me and moans out a strangled, "Please."

I pull my hand back just a bit, then slap the roundest part of her ass. Her knees start to buckle and she asks for more. "Harder this time," she breathes. I pull back further and come down harder, faster, causing a beautiful pink flush to appear. I squeeze the reddened skin, then rub soothing strokes to ease the sting. Without any warning to her, I grip her hips, pulling her up on the tips of her toes, and thrust into her. Deep, hard, quick thrusts as I support every bit of her weight.

The sounds of our bodies connecting beats like a melody in my ears. Her heavy breaths, my groans, skin against skin. The faster the beat of the music our bodies make, the closer I am to the edge. And when her walls tighten around me once, twice, *fuck.* My hips stutter, she pushes back against me, driving me deeper and we ride the wave of pleasure, together, right into oblivion. Slowly, gently, I slide out and back in, the head of my cock as sensitive as an exposed nerve. I give her ass a light smack when I pull all the way out of her. She whines at the absence of me then turns to place a quick and gentle kiss on my lips. I press my forehead against hers and breathe her in. The smells of sweat and sex linger in the air but she still smells like cinnamon. *I could get used to this.*

##

Charlie tried to save as many ornaments as she could from the dried-out dough, adding water in an attempt to bring it back to life. She managed to revive a few but not enough to really fill the tree, so while she set back to work making more, I searched for a sewing kit. A tiny, clear, plastic box with needles and thread and a few errant buttons sat perched on a shelf in the linen closet near where I'd found the strings of lights.

I popped popcorn for garland and grabbed the cranberries from the fridge. Charlie was surprised at my ability to quickly thread a needle. I refuse to tell her how many times I've had to sew my own clothes, especially making repairs or additions to my fatigues.

My five-to-one ratio of popcorn to cranberry seems to make her happy. At least, I think it's the homemade garland putting that smile on her face. Though I'd like to think that my tongue and my cock at least had a hand in that. Pretty sure it's the same for the gorgeous pink flush in her cheeks. *Stop staring. You'll give her a complex. She should know how beautiful she is. My very own personal Christmas angel. Well, not mine. But, maybe...? Go back to the garland, man. You keep looking at her like this and... ow!* I stab my thumb with the needle, too busy watching Charlie to notice I'd made it more than through the cranberry. I suck the spot on my thumb, unable to tell if the red on my skin is juice or blood. When I look a second time, my skin is stained but no evidence of active blood loss.

The sound of her giggle fills the air around me. I'll do anything to keep hearing that laugh. I toss a handful of popcorn at her and her answering jaw drop has me biting my tongue to keep from telling her to get on her knees and let me put that open mouth to good use. Good thing the countertop covers the swelling happening in my lap because these stupid sweatpants do me no favors. That's not something I've had to worry much about in the last couple of years. But damn if she doesn't find a way to wake the little guy up daily. Multiple times a day. *Don't say what you're thinking.*

"I wasn't kidding earlier; I really haven't made decorations for a Christmas tree since grade school. Is the five-to-one ratio okay?" I ask, trying anything to get my mind off taking her back into the bedroom and going for another round.

"I think that's perfect. Not too many cranberries, which means I can bake with what's left, and plenty of popcorn to give it a nice, full look. Popcorn garland on a tree reminds me of snow on the branches. White and thick and..." She bites her lower lip.

Uh oh. Are we still talking about popcorn? Change the subject before you look like a horny teenager.

"Tell me something I don't know about you." *Not what face you make when you orgasm, because I've seen that first hand and it's like looking directly into Heaven.* "Something you like or hate or love. Something someone would only know if they'd been inside the space in which you live." She thinks for a moment then her face goes red. "Not something embarrassing," I offer.

"Most people don't come over to my house. If they did, they would probably think I'm a little old lady trapped in a... *younger* woman's body." She puts serious emphasis on the "younger" part and I stifle a laugh. She's got to be at least 5 years younger than me and she looks even younger than that.

"27 cats?"

"What? No!" she nearly shouts. "You know how grandmas sometimes amass collections of knickknacks? Yeah, that's me. Curio cabinets, floating shelves, the whole shebang. All full. I like to pick up something from everywhere I've been. A tiny Statue of Liberty from New York, a miniature Golden Gate Bridge from San Francisco, a small, silver Eiffel Tower, among many many other things, to mark my time in Paris. In fact, Paris has its own curio cabinet. Things I can look at and remember exactly what part of the city I was in when I got them," she closes her eyes as if she's being transported directly to the cities she's talking about. A small smile creeps across her lips. "Each shop I walked into, the way it smelled, the things I saw, what time of day it was... I can remember everything." She opens her eyes again to find me staring at her, a smile of my own plastered on my face.

The sunshine in her soul pours out in beautiful rays and lights up the darkest parts of me. It's breathtaking, intoxicating, and entirely contagious. She's made me a better man in seven days than I've been able to do for myself in seven *months*. I've been trapped before. Stuck in places where there was seemingly no way out. But I can't say I've ever been in a situation quite like this. Two weeks trapped in a cabin with a stranger sounded like Hell when I first got here. Now? I don't ever want to leave. *I gotta remember to call George and tell him thank you for the best mistake he's ever made.*

Chapter Eight
Charlie
Day 10

The Christmas tree limbs were looking a bit droopy this morning so I made sure to fill the stand with water. As I stepped back, I admired the ornaments we made. Cute little barely decorated candy canes and wreaths hung from the branches with bits of thread. Tristan's popcorn garland was just starting to shrivel a smidge. The sheer simplicity of the decorations made the whole thing all the more beautiful. I sat down on the couch and waited for Tristan to finish cooking breakfast.

The last few nights, he's slept in the bedroom with me instead of on this couch. He wasn't on board at first. In fact, when he didn't follow me the first night, my heart hurt. We'd had this *mind-blowing* sex for the first time only hours before but at bedtime, he told me goodnight and laid down on the couch. Quietly, I retreated to the bedroom. I tossed and turned for a solid half hour before I couldn't take it anymore. I can't help but poke the bear. Throwing the covers off and bounding out of bed, I stomped my way into the living room. He was lying on the couch, reading something on his phone.

"Get your ass in here," I said, crossing my arms over my chest.

He sat up straight and stared at me for a moment before finally speaking. "I didn't want to assume. This isn't something we've talked about and I don't want you to feel uncomfortable or worse, obligated to invite me in your space."

"You could've asked. You can't just bend a girl over a counter and fuck her like that then leave her in bed alone later that night," I said with a huff.

"No ma'am, I don't think you can," he said as he stood to his feet with a grin on his face. He walked over to me and gently pressed a kiss to my forehead. "Would you like me to sleep in the bed with you, Charlie?"

I poked out my bottom lip, "Yes."

He smiled one of those genuine smiles I was starting to kind of, sort of, love a little. The ones that touch his eyes and relax his face. Then he led me into the bedroom. We didn't get much sleep that night. And each night since, he's come to bed on his own or dragged *me* with him instead.

Today, I want to pick his brain. We have a Christmas tree with no presents underneath. It's not like I can run into town and pick something up for him at the store.

One, it dumped snow on us again last night, no one is going anywhere today. And two, I wouldn't know what to get him anyway. Sure, I know him in the Biblical sense now, but I don't *know* him. We've talked about a few deeper things here and there but neither of us made a Christmas wish list. So, the only thing I know to do is what I do best: bake.

Tristan brings me a plate loaded with scrambled eggs, sausage, and bacon. He places a small metal bowl holding slices of buttered toast on the coffee table then goes back to the kitchen for two glasses of orange juice. Finally, he drops down onto the couch next to me and starts shoveling large bites from his plate into his mouth. I watch in stunned silence as the man cleans his plate in record time.

"How do you not have heartburn constantly?" I ask, truly concerned for his health at this point.

He shrugs, "How do you not weigh 500 pounds with all the sweets you taste test?"

My jaw drops. "Rude. But a valid point. Still. Slow down. It's okay to taste your food."

He chuckles, settling back into the couch as he downs his glass of orange juice.

"Tell me something," I start. He glares at me with a raised eyebrow. "What was your favorite holiday dessert growing up? What was the one thing you looked forward to seeing on your family's Christmas dessert table?"

He strokes the scruff on his face. The scratchy sounds fill the silence while he contemplates. "Hmm, if I had to choose one, I would say the peanut butter thumbprint cookies we all used to make with my grandma."

"But isn't that more for the memory of making them with her than the cookies themselves?" I challenge.

"Sure, it used to be. But ever since she passed, the cookies have been a reminder. I have her recipe taped to the inside of a cabinet door at home. I used to make them at Christmas, you know, to feel close to her. But a few years in a row, I went out on ops at Christmastime and couldn't make them. After that, I just... stopped altogether." His expression turns sad, his eyebrows knitting together.

"Did you fill the thumbprints with jam or jelly?" My question is partially out of curiosity and partially because I'm trying not to reach over and physically unfurl his eyebrows myself.

"Do you think that us kids would've begged her to make them every year if we did?" he asks with a chuckle.

I laugh, "Probably not. But if not jam, what did she fill the wells with?"

"Chocolate kisses," he answers quickly.

"Why am I not surprised?"

He gives me a gentle shove backward onto the couch and I nearly drop my plate. Good thing I've at least eaten the majority of it now. I place my plate on the coffee table and laugh. *It won't be the same recipe as his grandma used to make. Not unless I want to be completely obvious and pick his brain for a recipe he probably doesn't remember down to the exact measurements. Dammit, I didn't bring that bag of chocolate kisses with me. But I still have chocolate chips. Maybe. Unless Tristan's eaten them all by now. I caught him eating handfuls straight from the bag yesterday afternoon. I can make icing that'll be stiff enough... I'll make something else stiff later.* I pull my bottom lip between my teeth. Tristan cocks his head to the side and gives a sly smile.

"Something you'd like to share with the class?" he questions.

My mouth goes dry, heat pooling in the space between my legs. If all this man gives me for Christmas is his beautiful cock, I'll be more than satisfied. If this, two weeks trapped in a cabin with him, the way he appreciates every inch of my body, the respect he shows me, the care he gives–if this is my Christmas present, then I'm a happy girl. When I first met him, I was certain he was either going to murder me in my sleep or I'd wake up one morning and he'd simply be gone. Ten days ago I wouldn't have believed that we'd be sitting on the couch together, laughing like this, and one word away from ripping each other's clothes off. I would've called anyone crazy who dared try telling me this was a possibility.

"No, I think I'll keep this one to myself. For now," I state matter-of-factly. His sly smile all but disappears.

I jump from the couch and set off to the linen closet. I need something to distract us both. Alright, mostly me. Because if I sit this close to him any longer without something between us, I will straddle him and ride him like a bull. And we can't just spend all day, every day, the rest of our time here having sex... *can we? No, no. Do something else first.*

I dig around in the linen closet, searching the shelves for the one thing all vacation spots have in common: games. Board games, a cribbage set, a deck of cards. *Strip poker, anyone? Charlie, you're going to get yourself into all sorts of trouble.* The one way to really get to know someone is to play a game with them. It's an activity that will either make the two of you or break you into pieces. Considering Tristan has spent every day so far teaching me a little more about self-defense and I've turned it into a game of, "Can I Flip The Lumbersnack?" this might actually be what breaks us. I may or may not be a *tiny* bit competitive. I find a cribbage set that's obviously missing pieces, a chess board missing two rooks, and two decks of cards. I grab the cards and before I shut the door, I see Clue sitting on the top shelf. *Nope, no way. I will lose my ass trying to play Clue with Mr. Detective.*

Dropping down into the floor in front of the fireplace, I pat the empty space across from me then toss the decks of cards in between. Tristan's face twists into a look of confusion. "You can't tell me you've never played any card games. I refuse to accept that," I say.

"Oh, I've played plenty," he answers, sliding off the couch and onto the floor to sit cross-legged in front of me. "Five card stud? Hold'em? Strip poker? Please tell me we're betting articles of clothing. No one loses."

See! It's not just me. I clear my throat, suddenly too warm, and stretch one leg out to the side. "I was thinking something more along the lines of..." I pull the cards from their sleeve and shuffle while I stare into his eyes. "Slapjack!"

"Really? You really want to try me?" He cuts the air with his hands in some wild, crazy, karate move so fast my vision blurs. "Your tiny ninja ass is no match for me. Sit there and learn something, grasshopper." The smile that tugs on his lips is adorable.

"You haven't seen my moves yet," I say with a sassy flip of my hair. "At least, not these." I deal twenty-six cards to each of us and watch as he rubs his hands together, blowing into them.

Tristan lays down the first card: a four of hearts. I lay down the seven of clubs for the second card. We go back and forth, laying down card after card, both of us twitching in anticipation for the reveal of the first Jack. And when it comes, I'm the one who plays it: Jack of Spades. But despite my hand hovering over the cards, I'm not quick enough to slap the pile of cards first. Tristan's lightning reflexes win out and what I slap instead of the cards is the back of his hand. He smiles up at me, sliding the pile of cards to his side of the floor.

"Okay, I'll give you that one."

He smiles, returning his hand to the facedown stack of cards he's holding with the other, eager to turn the next one.

I go first this time: Ace of diamonds. His turn brings the nine of diamonds to the pile. Back to the seesaw we go, trading off low-numbered cards and the odd Queen or King before finally making it to the next Jack. This time I don't miss a beat when I turn the card over to see a Jack staring me in the face. My hand drops so fast, I'm not sure Tristan had time to see if it was even a Jack at all.

"Damn," he says under his breath. He adjusts his shoulders and readies himself for the next round. He drops a three of hearts on the floor first and I immediately follow it up with an eight of spades. More trading off higher numbered cards this time before the third Jack. Our hands hit the pile at the exact same time, our heads snapping up to meet each other's narrowed eyes.

"Nuh-uh, no way. This is mine," I claim.

"Fat fucking chance. My hand was clearly down first," he scoffs.

All at once, and with zero forethought, I lunge across the pile of cards, right into his lap. The force of my movement should've knocked him backward. The only time I have anything close to an upper hand is when he's caught off guard. But this time, this time I don't move him a bit. He catches me and laughs. My eyes are wide as he effortlessly pins me to the ground beside him. Realization hits that I've never truly caught him off guard. Not once. He let me think I had the advantage. *Confidence is killer.*

His laughter is loud and the more he laughs, the less I can keep it together. It's a struggle to get free of his grip but I make it. He wipes at his eyes and I give him a playful shove, actually moving him now.

He catches his breath and says, "If it really means that much to you, you can have the pile." He holds up his cards to show that he's got well over three-quarters of the deck already. I was down to my last few cards before that Jack was thrown. The competitive side of me wants to take it. When I hesitate, Tristan holds his cards up, bending them between his thumb and fingers. "Or we could just play Fifty-Two Card Pick up." He lets the cards fly into the air, reds, and blacks cascading down to the floor around us. Tristan leans in and catches my lips with his as the last couple of cards fall. Somehow, we'd managed to not let the game break us. But we'd done enough of the something else for me. Now it's time to have a little afternoon fun.

Chapter Nine
Tristan
Christmas Eve

Christmas Eve was finally here and I hadn't had much to work with in terms of getting Charlie something she really might have wanted. To be honest, I hadn't asked what she wanted either. It didn't matter all that much given that I wasn't going to leave to get her anything. She'd said she bought knickknacks to mark the time she spent in different places. Well, I spent a lot of hurry-up and wait time on ops in different places doing fuck all, so I perfected some wood carving techniques. My best bet at putting a smile on her face for Christmas was to carve her something to remember this place by. To remember *me* by. Hopefully, it would mark a beautiful memory, one that was only the beginning of a lifetime full of memories and knickknacks to come.

Last night, I found a roll of Christmas paper in the linen closet that keeps on giving. Guests must leave things often and George just stashes them away in the closet for the next person with an odd need. The red, white, and green striped paper looked like it was intended for Christmas wrapping. I'd carefully wrapped the carving in the paper and tied it up with thread after I spent half an hour looking for tape and catching Charlie's attention one too many times. Then I'd quietly tucked it under the tree without her noticing. The wooden recreation of the cabin didn't feel like nearly enough for someone as deserving of the world as Charlie, but it would have to do for now. I promised myself I'd get her something even better once we made it back to civilization. *I'll take her out to dinner somewhere fancy. Somewhere she can trust the chef, sit back and relax, have a nice meal cooked for her by someone that really knows what they're doing and doesn't just get by on luck.* Our story is only just beginning.

I woke up early this morning. Charlie was cuddled up next to me, her arm draped over my side. A small smile played on her lips, and when I pressed a light kiss to her forehead, she sighed. She's the angel I needed all along. I quietly slid out of bed and started up both fireplaces. Though I would've rather kept Charlie warm with my body heat, she had been up early and made breakfast the last few days. It was my turn. And this morning will, hopefully, be special. The Conrad family tradition was always Santa pancakes on Christmas morning. I hadn't made them in years but they weren't difficult. I threw together pancake batter and promptly burned the first pancake. Then the second. The third, however, turned out a nice, golden brown.

It's a good thing I had planned to make these for myself and brought a can of whipped cream. It's also a good thing Charlie isn't awake to see me *using* said whipped cream and not making it myself. I arrange slices of strawberries in a triangle shape at the top and spray an outline of whipped cream. A strawberry slice for each rosy cheek, chocolate chips of course for the eyes, and more whipped cream for Santa's beard. I set the can on the counter and admire my work. *It looks sort of like Santa. Sort of. Oh, she's going to hate this. I should scrap all of it. There are plenty more pancakes I didn't burn. I could just give her those and forget about this whole Santa face thing. Not sure that's even possible. This shit will probably haunt me in my sleep.* I pour a glass of orange juice and fill a second glass with water then gather it all to carry into the bedroom.

Charlie stirs when I accidentally clink the glasses together as I place them on the nightstand. "Good morning, sleepyhead," I say as she turns to look at me, barely opening one eye. "Merry Christmas Eve."

She groans, stretching her arms above her head. She pulls the covers tightly to her as she sits up in bed. "What'd you do?" she asks in an adorable sleepy voice that makes me want to crawl back into bed with her.

I smile, handing her the plate, "I made a traditional Conrad family Christmas breakfast. This is what my mom made every Christmas Eve morning when we were kids. Thought I would restart the tradition this year."

She gathers whipped cream on her finger and pops it into her mouth, licking it clean as she stares at me. "We don't have whipping cream," she states, eyeing me carefully.

I shake my head, lightly laughing at her expression. "No, we don't. But this will do." I point at her plate and notice I forgot a fork. Hurriedly, I grab two forks and toss a couple of pancakes on a plate for myself with a handful of chocolate chips and a quick shot of whipped cream. The strawberries smelled so good while I was cutting them, I couldn't resist the urge to pop a couple of them in my mouth on my way back to Charlie. She thanked me when I handed her the fork and I plopped down on the bed beside her.

"How come yours doesn't look like… Santa?" she asks, her head cocked to the side as if she doesn't understand why my plate looks normal while hers looks like a kindergarten craft project gone horribly wrong.

"Not enough time for fancy presentation." With my fork, I rearrange the chocolate chips to look like eyes. "There. Now my food can stare back at me too."

She giggles then cuts into her pancakes, dips them in whipped cream, and stabs a strawberry to complete the bite. Charlie glares at me when I add a chocolate chip from my own plate onto the bite as she brings it to her mouth. "Sorry," I mouth.

Her eyes close and she hums low in her throat. *You did good after all, T-Rex.* We eat the rest of breakfast in comfortable silence. When we've finished, I watch as she stands from bed, as naked as the first time I laid eyes on her, and sashays her way to the kitchen. My cock stands at attention. The thought of her full, perky breasts hanging over the sink as she does the dishes entirely in the nude floods every corner of my mind. I adjust the tent in my sweatpants, tucking the head of my dick into my waistband in hopes to conceal, for now, just how turned on she makes me.

Peering around the corner, I watch as she rinses our plates and places them in the drainboard next to the sink. Of course she catches me staring and a delicious smile starts to spread. She's fucking beautiful. In clothes, or out of them, she's relaxed and confident. I'm not sure how I was lucky enough to have my wish come true but damn if I won't do everything I can to hold onto it. *In fact...* There's no way to keep my hands off her when she looks like this. I step behind her and place a hand on one hip, moving her hair away from her neck with the other. Light kisses to the top of her shoulder are all it takes to make her moan. Goosebumps rise on her arms and neck as my lips brush against her ear. *Fuck, I'd take her right here in the kitchen again. But we agreed last night to pause the hanky panky until this evening. Damn, she smells good; like cinnamon and clean skin.* More kisses down her neck and before I know it, my hand has wandered from her hip to the very wet, very warm spot between her legs.

"Tristan," she moans. "Not yet." She turns to face me, effectively stopping the crawl of my fingers up to her entrance. A quick kiss on my lips is all I get before she swishes her hips right into the bedroom. I palm my erection through my pants. The way my cock aches to be inside her is something I don't remember feeling ever before. For anyone. But it's more than that. And I need to tell her everything. *Open and honest communication is key. That's what my therapist says. With Piper, I always kept the door of communication closed. Sealed that fucker shut with every nail and screw I could find. I won't do that again. Not with Charlie. I won't take this for granted.*

We spent the rest of the morning and into the afternoon lounging around watching more Christmas movies and drinking the battlefield special. Knowing there's only one more day of this, her in my arms, cuddled on the couch watching corny-ass Christmas movies that we both love, is beginning to put me in a funk. Instead of sulking about it, I made the conscious effort to hug her a little tighter, plant a few extra kisses on the top of her head, and soak in the smell of her skin.

When the third movie ends, she jumps up off the couch. "Do *not* look. No matter what sounds you hear, what you smell, nothing. You do not look. And if I catch you staring, your ass is grass. I'll send you outside with the snow."

"Not even a little peek?" I tease. It would be impossible for her to force me out the door, but I wouldn't put it past her to try with all her might. Her answering glare lets me know I'm pushing my luck. I'm starting to get that look from her regularly but with the way it makes my cock twitch, I don't think it's having the effect she desires.

I used the last of the firewood this morning so since she wants me out of her hair, I decide to make myself useful. With my hand shielding my sight, I retreat to the bedroom for warmer clothes and repeat the process on my way out the front door. Charlie is in the zone; all manner of baking ingredients littering the counter around her. Yes, I snuck a peek. Sue me.

Outside, the snow has started melting under the heat of the sun making the gravel driveway visible for the first time since we've been here. The group of trees behind the cabin that I've been slowly hacking at for almost two weeks still holds enough trees that it could lose a few more and be fine. I trudge in the slushy, melting piles of snow back to the grouping of evergreens. The now drooping branches, hanging heavy with the weight of melted snow, mirror the creeping weight of sadness that we'll soon be heading back to the real world. Our time left here is as short as this tree stump will be when I'm finished. I give the tree closest to me a few solid whacks, the wood splitting the way I can already feel my heart tearing in two. I'm not ready to lose this closeness with her. I said I wasn't going to sulk, but I'm alone out here now and it's hard as hell not to sink into the thoughts Charlie was having just a few days ago. *What happens when we leave here? Are we in a relationship now? Is this all we get; this place, these walls, these two weeks? It can't be. I want her to meet Lil and Knox. They'd love her. I want to spend my nights with her just like we have here, cooking dinner together, sharing meals, and swapping stories. It can't end. I'll move mountains to be with her. I just hope she feels the same way.*

Once I'm done cutting the logs, I tuck them under my arms and head back to the cabin. Charlie's head snaps up when I walk in the door.

"Don't look!" she yells, throwing her body over the counter to shield whatever she baked. Apparently, that wasn't the smartest idea considering how fast she raises up. She dances around, fanning the front of her body, a pained expression on her face.

"Charlie, are you okay?" I ask, the wood clattering to the floor as I rush to her side.

She bounces around a second longer before blowing out a sharp breath and smoothing her shirt. "Okay, I'm good. I'm good. Wait!" She quickly covers my eyes with her hands. "You can't see them yet! They're not finished!"

I pry her hands from my face and look her over. "Whatever it is that you're making is the least of my worries right now." Her arms don't show any visible signs of burns and aside from being extremely flustered, she seems perfectly fine. Her bottom lip disappears between her teeth and I gently kiss her forehead. "Okay, now, can I see what it is you're making?"

She steps back slightly and motions over the counter. I'm met with at least three dozen, small, round cookies with divots in the middle and cracked edges. *Thumbprint cookies.* "You made these for me?" A whole host of emotions begins to well up behind my eyes. I take in a deep breath before I look at her.

Charlie's eyes are glassy as she says, "Well, they're not done yet. And *someone* ate the chocolate kisses, but there were still chocolate chips left and I figured I would use them as a substitute. I know they won't be exactly like the ones you used to make with your grandma but..."

The memories of Grandma Jean's kitchen flood my mind. Small and cozy, a lot like this one, with red and white checked wallpaper. It always smelled like freshly baked bread, the way it smelled in here after Charlie baked those quick rolls our first night. Bright and warm, full of love and joy. It was the place I felt the most safe. The most loved. When I was out on ops, Grandma Jean's kitchen was the place I wanted to make it back to. I close my eyes and her sweet, smiling face is right there, shining with pride as she hands me chocolate kisses to fill the wells of the cookies. I open my eyes again, firmly back in reality, and take Charlie in my arms. Charlie, without even knowing, had just given me the best present I'd ever received.

Chapter Ten
Charlie
Christmas Eve

"Thank you, Charlie," he says, hugging me tighter. "Really. I mean it." He reaches for a cookie, and I swat his hand.

"No, sir." I hand him the chocolate chips and dig out a handful. Then I start filling with the wells in the tops of the peanut butter cookies with a few chips in each. The warmth of the cookie starts to melt the chocolate and he stares at me as he adds chips into a few of them himself. "Fine, you can have one now," I say. No sooner than the words leave my mouth, the man pops two cookies, one after another, into his mouth. The satisfied hum low in his throat makes almost seriously burning myself more than worth it.

"God, these are good," he mumbles through the mouthful. He's adorable when he allows himself to be this relaxed. Not that he isn't hot as hell when he's being stoic and gruff, because, let's face it, that's what drew me to him in the first place. But this softer side of him, I could get used to it too. *Haven't I already?*

I've gotten used to waking up to his smile, falling asleep in his arms, cooking dinner with or for him, or watching him cook for me. Yes, I've even gotten used to letting go of some of the control. I'll miss our nights on the couch, watching Christmas movies, talking about anything under the sun. I'm going to miss his smile, his laugh, his... everything. But do I have to miss him at all? I don't. And I don't want to. I need to make that clear as day before we lose another second.

"Tristan," I start, but he quickly interrupts me.

"I know there's no way what I made for you is going to match up to this, but..." He walks over to the Christmas tree and kneels beside it, reaching behind the large branches to retrieve a small, wrapped package. I see that it's tied together with thread when he makes it back to the kitchen and hands it to me. I wasn't expecting him to make me anything, genuinely. I made him cookies with no expectations of anything in return, but I'd just about bet that he made whatever this is with the same thoughts. "I thought you might like something to remember us-... this trip by," he says, stumbling over the last bit.

Carefully, I remove the red, white, and green striped paper from the object. It isn't exactly heavy but it's not all that light either. It's a bit bigger than my hand as I remove the thread and paper from it and hold it up. It takes me a minute to realize what it is. Light-colored wood, complete with deeper brown knots, carved in the shape of a small building. This building. *The cabin!* The same tree that stands tall to the right side of the cabin, the chimney that pokes up from the roof, the rounded edges of the log walls, and he even captured the giant floor-to-ceiling windows on the side. And right in front of the door, a mound of what must be snow in exactly the same spot where the mound that toppled inside sat. It is *beautiful*. It captures so many memories. I can smell the crisp, cold air just looking at it. This time, I can't hold back the tears and, silently, they slide down my cheeks.

"You hate it so much it made you cry. I'm so sorry, I promise I'll get you something better the second we get back to town," he rambles. I place the carving on the counter in the only clean spot and wrap my arms around his neck, pulling him tightly to me.

"Thank you," I whisper between soft sobs. "It's perfect."

His very rigid shoulders relax as he sighs in relief. "I really will get you anything you want the very minute we're back home," he promises.

I pull back to look him in the eyes. Those warm, doe eyes that pull me in deep and hold me there. "There is nothing money can buy that would ever top this. Nothing." Thoughts of his eyes as big as saucers when I flew out of the shower at him, naked as the day I was born, dance in my memory. The amount of respect he showed me that night was something I'd never encountered. Getting through the grit of his grumpy exterior to find the sweet center underneath was a challenge I'd gladly take over and over again. "Thank you for letting me in, for taking a chance and not leaving. Thank you for choosing to make lemon bars with me," I say, wiping my eyes.

"Charlie, I should be thanking you," he says, taking my hands in his. "My whole world has been dark for so long and you, tiny ninja, came flying in and lit everything up. You set my world, my heart, my very soul on fire in a way I didn't even think was possible. I don't deserve a second of your time. I'm not worthy of breathing the same air you do." I open my mouth to scold him and he holds up a finger, "I know. That isn't how you see me. For a long time, I haven't thought I was worth much of anything. You're helping me change that. This last week, I've been trying like hell to see myself through your eyes instead. As a man who can be kind and gentle, invest in someone other than me, and be your safe place to land. I want to live up to that, to be that man for you every day. I don't want this to end when we go back home. If you'll have me, I'd like to take you out on a proper date. If the magic of this cabin wears off and I turn back into a pumpkin, I'll understand if you say no to a second one. But I'd like to give this a real shot. What do you say?"

The tears fall faster now, spilling over my cheeks. Tristan's brow furrows and he reaches to stop the flow. I feel like an idiot for crying instead of jumping in his arms and stealing every bit of breath from his lungs. I chuckle but it comes out a strangled mix of sobs and laughter. Relaxed and comfortable aren't things I typically feel. With a bakery to run entirely on my own, there's never time to take a break. The last two weeks with Tristan sharing the load, and well, the last week of him sharing *his* load, have been everything I needed and more. And now, the one thing I was the most worried about is nothing but an afterthought to the man standing in front of me. *He doesn't want this to end. He wants to go on a date. A real, honest to God, date. And another after that. Then a whole lifetime of finding knickknacks and making dinners together. Or arguing over who gets to do the dishes. Okay, I'm getting ahead of myself, but you can see it. Right? Yeah, if he thinks he's going to be a pumpkin in my eyes,* ever, *he's wrong.*

"Yes. Absolutely yes!" I realize a moment too late that I sound like I'm accepting a marriage proposal. But that doesn't matter to Tristan who scoops me into his arms and that stealing the air from his lungs thing...? He does it to me instead. There's an urgency in his kiss that sends waves of electricity pulsing through me all the way to my toes. The hard muscles of his chest press against me as he moves to deepen the kiss, his tongue pleading with my lips to part. I grant him access and our tongues dance in a rhythm that speaks directly to my soul. Every inch of me is alive, all for him. Before we can get carried away and the cookies I made end up on the floor, I break the kiss. The look on his face threatens to break my heart. You'd think I just told him I unalived his puppy. I reach up and stroke the stubble on his cheek. "There's plenty of time for more of that later. You're stuck with me, soldier," I breathe against his lips.

"Yes ma'am. And there's nowhere I'd rather be."

##

Hot cocoa, Battlefield Special style, and thumbprint cookies very well may have been all we had for dinner while we soaked up the last relaxing day of our trip. Movie after movie played in the background of deep conversations about Grandma Jean's kitchen with all of Tristan's cousins and my own grandmother's kitchen where I learned to love baking alongside my sister who despised it. We sat on that couch for hours, limbs tangled together like the strings of lights before we'd hung them on the Christmas tree. Tristan made me feel comfortable, relaxed, and most of all, he made me feel safe. Safe enough to fully be myself, safe enough to let go.

The male lead in our fourth Christmas movie of the night stretches to place the star on top of the Christmas tree and Tristan pulls me onto his lap. I let out a small squeal when he wraps me in his arms. His smile touches his eyes. "The movie, Tristan," I half-whimper.

"I'm only interested in watching one thing right now." He lifts me, turning to lay me on the couch. As he settles his hips between my legs, his eyes scan my body. "This will be like our own Christmas movie. There will be unwrapping," he says, tilting my chin to the side. "Unraveling," he breathes against my neck, kissing his way up. "Undoing," he whispers into my ear. My body tenses and relaxes at the same time. Tingling sensations spread across my skin quickly followed by goosebumps as the roughness of his few days old beard scratches against my neck. While my heart pounds and my breathing quickens, Tristan slips a hand underneath my shirt. The heat from his skin on mine sends a shiver rushing through me. Carefully, he tugs the shirt up and over my head.

"My God, Charlie," he breathes before leaning down to press small kisses to my now-exposed breasts. Those kisses trail across stiffened nipples and my back arches as I moan his name, "*Tristan...*"

He brushes his fingertips up my side and back down, catching the waistband of my pants with his forefinger and pulling them down just enough to fully uncover my hip bone. He's taking his time and it's driving me wild. The small bites to the skin at my hip and just below my waist, without even fully undressing me, are causing things between my legs to become slick. His eyes flick up to mine as he makes his way down further, peeling my yoga pants from my body at an achingly slow speed. My breath hitches watching him inch closer to my center, tongue taking the place of lips in a trail across my lower belly and down to that sweet spot. He flattens his tongue against it then drags lazily upward and my legs jerk, tightening around him. Tristan lets out a small laugh at the quick movement and the puff of warm breath on the sensitive spot sends my head backward.

Without warning, he changes positions, planting his face firmly between my legs and wrapping his arms around my thighs, the tips of his fingers digging in. He pulls me closer to him, surely cutting off his air supply as he buries his tongue inside me and the bridge of his nose rubs harshly against my clit. The vibrations from his moans of satisfaction are captivating; I have to see him. But the second I look down to find that he's watching me come apart, my legs shake, the muscles in my belly tighten and my walls clench around his tongue. I grip the back of the couch and try to hold on as fireworks explode behind my eyes. He rides it out with me, slowing the pace of his tongue before sliding it up and around my clit. The nerves there are now wholly electrified. The light nibbles and gentle sucking send a lightning-like response all the way to the tips of my toes.

Tristan trades his tongue for his finger, continuing the measured movements while working his way out of those grey sweats I've come to love. Breathless, a writhing mess underneath him, I watch as his hard length bobs, free from its former prison. "Too slow," I pant, pulling away from him. The look of surprise on his face is priceless and if I wasn't so focused on riding his cock, I would probably laugh. I need him; inside me, close to me, his skin to mine. I push against his shoulder, directing him to sit on the couch then straddle his lap. Taking his face in my hands, I crash my lips with his, tasting myself there.

A muted growl rumbles in his chest as I guide his cock to my entrance and slowly lower myself down onto him. Quickly, he pulls back from the kiss to watch as he enters me. "*Fuck, Charlie...*" he groans. He grips my hips and raises his own to meet me, driving himself so deep it almost hurts. A small whimper escapes my lips when he twists a hand in the hair at the nape of my neck and tugs my head closer to his. He presses his forehead to mine and I slowly begin to move, savoring every inch of him on the way up and back down. I let myself get lost in the feeling of him; the ridges of his cock against my walls, the tight fit, the pulsing of muscles clenching as each thrust drives us both closer to orgasm.

He wraps his arms around me, pressing skin to skin, quickening the pace from underneath. My nails dig into his back as I try to hold on; to him, to reality, to slow the lit fuse threatening to cause another explosion of fireworks. But I'm losing. Failing. And I don't care. I throw my head back as high-pitched moans between breaths come tumbling out of me as I fall right over the edge. The repeated clenching of my walls around his cock milks the orgasm from him and his entire body tenses. Burying his face in my chest, he moans against my skin as he comes. I keep rocking my hips, riding the last waves and enjoying every bit of the small jerks his legs make at the sensations.

"You're going to kill me, you know it?" he pants, staring into my eyes.

"At least you'll die a happy man," I state confidently, stealing a quick kiss before climbing off of him. His hand stays on my thigh, still draped across his lap, squeezing and rubbing it like he can't get enough. *I can't either.* I drag my fingertips along the back of his hand. We stay just like this, taking the time to recover, until Tristan springs from the couch and scoops me in his arms.

"Round two," he says. I hold onto his neck, giggling as he carries me to the bedroom.

After another round... and another... we lay in bed, arms, and legs tangled together. Tristan pushes the hair out of my face and pulls me to his chest. I breathe him in, snuggling as close as I can. I feel the smile stretch across his face as he kisses the top of my head. My eyes are heavy and sleep is coming faster than I'd like. As I drift off, I hear Tristan sleepily whisper, "Wonder how we'll ever top this Christmas."

Chapter Eleven
Tristan
Christmas Morning...?

Buzz! Buzz! An annoying yet familiar sound pulls me from sleep. I give the black box on my nightstand a good smack, silencing the noise then turn back to my side to wrap my arms around... *a pillow?* I sit bolt upright in bed, heart pounding in my chest. "Charlie!?" My vision blurry, I search the mattress, the comforter, between the sheets, for any sign of her and come up empty. No clothes I'd taken off her last night, not a bit of her was here in my bed. *My bed... The cabin?* The fight for understanding is a desperate one. And one that I am certain I'm losing. *I was at the cabin, in bed, with Charlie. It was Christmas Eve...* My phone vibrates, rattling against the wooden nightstand. The lock screen shows a very different story than my current understanding.

December 11 - Office Christmas Party

Right there, in big, bold letters, a calendar notification makes it perfectly clear that something has gone horribly wrong. I spring from bed and run to the kitchen. *Maybe she's there. Cooking breakfast like she has the last five mornings in a row. You can't tell me I dreamed all of that.* Standing in my empty kitchen, I touch my lips, still able to feel the soft velvet of hers when I think about the last kiss we shared before we drifted off to sleep. *No way that wasn't real.* My last chance at holding on to any bit of hope comes crashing down when I search my neck in the bathroom mirror. She marked me two nights ago, a huge hickey right above my collarbone like we were a couple of lovesick teenagers. Finding nothing, no mark, no bruise, no sign of her on my skin in my reflection, I sink to my knees on the bathroom floor.

If all of it was a dream, it has to have meant something. *God, it's a good thing I see a therapist regularly. I just spent an entire two weeks with someone in a damn dream.* But that someone changed me. That someone made me open up, think about someone else's feelings, put someone else first. She made me feel alive again. I wished for a do-over and I got it. Not once, but twice. *I just have to find Charlie.* I pull myself together, standing to my feet and staring at myself in the mirror once more. "Alright T-Rex," I tell the man staring back at me, "It's time to shake some shit up."

After I shower and get dressed, I head back to the kitchen for some coffee. When I open the cabinet door, an avalanche of coffee pods tumble out and I quickly catch the flask that falls with them. Chuckling to myself, I place the flask back in the cabinet and forego the Irish coffee, remembering Lil's twisted expression two weeks ago. *Well, I guess, tonight. Oh, that means... I already met the airhe-... woman Lil set me up with. The blind date. She's a treat. She's no Charlie, that's for sure.* I snap a pod into the coffee maker and wait while the warm liquid fills my travel mug.

Charlie. I have to talk to her. What if she remembers too? Okay, but what if she doesn't? And I freak her the fuck out. I pick up my phone to find her number and give her a call only to realize after scrolling that I don't have it. *Of course not. She doesn't give me her number for another two weeks. Well, that won't do. What did she say the name of her bakery was again?* "Sweet Temptations!" I shout at the empty space. A quick web search gives me the store's phone number but before I can call, my phone vibrates with a text message.

Knox: Hey man, you coming in today or what? I can't sift through these new recruit files alone.

You don't sift through shit. You hide off in the break room today and bullshit with the guys until it's time to leave and pick up Lil. Oh, she's going to expect me to bring something tonight and she won't be happy when I show up empty-handed. Dynamite comes in small packages and I'd rather not light the fuse. The guys would be happy with a couple of 30-packs but, boom goes the dynamite. I know she has most of the food taken care of but what if...

I fire a text back to Knox, letting him know I'll be a bit later than I thought and to get started without me–*that'll happen*–then open my browser again to pull up the number for the bakery. I wait while the line rings, then *she* picks up.

"Sweet Temptations, this is Charlie! How can I make your holiday merry and bright?" She nearly sings the words, her voice as bright as the smile I can hear behind them. *Oh shit. Say something. Anything.* Fucking crickets. "Hello? Anybody still there? I heard you breathing just a few seconds ago."

I end the call, dropping my phone on the kitchen table. *What an idiot. All you had to do was say hi. Say anything, really. It didn't have to be anything like, "Hey, do you remember spending two weeks trapped in a cabin with me? Because I remember the way you taste." I can't just talk to her over the phone. I need to see her. I need to get lost in those beautiful eyes.* Before I even realize what I'm doing, I grab my keys and head for the door. *Shit.* Turning around, I swipe my coffee mug from the counter.

The bakery isn't far from the office, so I park my truck in the office lot and set off walking. Two blocks in the crisp, cold air will do my head some good. Maybe it'll keep me from making a complete ass of myself and spill that my life just turned into a reverse version of Back to the Future. I cross to the other side of the street, passing a restaurant I used to frequent and it hits me. I didn't wake up this morning torturing myself with memories of Piper. Hell, I haven't thought about her *once* in days. *Wow. I believe that's called progress.*

I round the corner of Peach and Second Street and a knot begins to form in my gut. *Nerves? That's new.* I've never been one to be nervous about anything. You kind of have to stay as calm and collected as humanly possible in my career field. Especially in my former job with the military. But here I am, shaking like a leaf and it isn't due to the cold. I want with every fiber of my being for this to go right. I *need* it to go right. Charlie Blaine flew into my life and I'll move Heaven and Earth to make sure she doesn't fly right back out.

The bakery, tucked neatly between two larger buildings, comes into view as I walk onto Main Street. An adorable white sign that reads "Sweet Temptations" in one of those cutesy fonts hangs over the door. She even has a couple of sections of white picket fencing on either side of her building separating her from the cold, grey cement blocks of her neighbors. It looks wildly out of place but the line outside the door shows just how much she stands out; the building and the baker herself. Hardly stopping to check for cars, I jog across the street and take my place at the back of the line. The number of people willing to stand in the cold and wait is staggering. If there's nothing left by the time I finally make it inside, that's fine. I'm not here for her baked goods as much as I am here for her. Less than a handful of people pour out of the shop and the line moves up.

Two people file in line behind me, chatting with each other about how wonderful the lemon blueberry muffins are at this place. Their breath, along with anyone else who dares open their mouth in the frigid air, comes out in visible puffs. Someone ahead of me mentions that as soon as they see Charlie, they're telling her it's time to expand. I chuckle to myself. *She would never allow anyone else in a kitchen to represent her. You get her or you get nothing. It's not haughty, in my opinion.* I can't, however, say that most people freezing their asses off in this line would agree. The line moves up again and I'm two people away from the door.

When I make it inside, my senses are overtaken by the sweet smells of vanilla and freshly baked cookies. The glass cases are all empty, save for one box of cookies. And there she is. Charlie Blaine, cheery and warm when she says, "Merry Happy Holidays! Welcome to Sweet Temptations! I'm sorry, I've only got a dozen cookies left!" The two people behind me who stuck out the cold just as long as I did sighed heavily before turning to leave. "Next time, I guess," one of them mumbles under their breath. I'm utterly mesmerized by Charlie. Her eyes are green today and the smile she wears is the same wattage of brightness as the one she wore when I plugged in the lights on our Christmas tree. Her deep red sweater hugs each and every curve in just the right way.

"Sir?" she questions when I still haven't spoken a word.

"No need for the formalities," I joke, repeating a line I'd said to her on our first full day at the cabin. The sound of her soft laugh is melodic. "I'll take the whole dozen, please."

She beams brightly, boxing up the dozen cookies in neatly crimped, dark green paper before tucking them into a bright red box.

Say something else. Ask her how she's doing, what her plans are for Christmas. Or...

"Do you have plans tonight?"

She blinks quickly, my abrupt question catching her off guard. She eyes me carefully. *Right, Charlie's never met me before.* I catch sight of large coffee makers behind her. "Let me start over. I'd like a cup of coffee, please, and if you have time, some company to drink it with."

Her cheeks flush that rosy pink color. I've seen it enough times now to know the difference between embarrassment and arousal. This is the latter. "Say yes,

Charlie," I say, leaning forward and resting my crossed arms on the glass counter.

"How do you... Do I know you?" she asks quietly. Her eyes search my face then trail down my body and the pink flush deepens. She grabs a coffee mug and pours until it's full.

"Not yet, but you will." I give her a sly smile. Watching as she turns to pour another cup, I notice the black yoga pants she's wearing. *She* does *live in those things.* She rounds the corner and points at one of the small tables for me to sit down. I do as instructed, more than ready to ask her all the questions I already know the answers to. We've done this before. Well, not *this* exactly, but the awkward getting-to-know-you part–we have that down pat. I just want to kiss her again. Before she joins me, she locks the door. I decide against making a joke about her holding me hostage.

We spent the next three hours talking like old friends. It felt somewhat like cheating to know what I did so I spent a solid hour asking questions about her family, her time in Paris and Germany, and the cost of upkeep on a building like this in the heart of downtown. She spent an hour grilling me on my time with the SEALs, asking careful questions out of genuine curiosity. The last hour, we talked about what we'd like to do differently in the New Year.

"I want to expand," she says, much to my surprise. "I haven't told anyone. I'm shutting down the shop for two weeks to go on vacation and the hit to my income is significant. If I could let go of some of the control, I wouldn't have to worry about that." She stares out the window a moment, taking the last sip of her coffee. "The line out the door today, and at least every other day, is a reminder that I've done my job well, but also that I can't keep running this as a one-woman show."

I realized then that I hadn't seen a single staff member since I came in. *She's had no help and her typical business day looks like that? No wonder she was so exhausted at the cabin. I should have rubbed her feet every day.* "I think I'd start with hiring some people to help here before you look into expansion. Your plate is already overflowing."

She nods her head, "You're right. That's what this vacation is about. Forcing myself to relax, take a breath, spend some time in the middle of nowhere, and just be. Step outside of my comfort zone. Because as wild as it may sound, I'm the most comfortable here in the chaos."

Whoops. Well, you might be a tiny bit busy some of that time. But there will be plenty of chaos, tiny ninja.

"I know what that's like, not wanting to let someone else handle your business for you. My partner, Knox, is taking care of things while I go on vacation myself and

I'm a little concerned I won't have an office to come back to," I chuckle. *Stepping out of your comfort zone is tough. But Charlie made me want to try. And when I did, it was beautiful. She's beautiful.* "Speaking of the office, do you have plans tonight? Besides packing for your trip, of course."

Charlie places her mug on the table and wraps her pretty little fingers around the sides and locks those hazel eyes onto mine. There's a hint of a sparkle to them when she asks, "What did you have in mind?"

Charlie gave me her address and I told her that I'd pick her up around 1800 hours. She laughed as she counted from twelve to figure out I meant six o'clock. I made it to her apartment at a quarter til and waited before I knocked. When she opened the door, I was met with a set of honeyed eyes that stopped my heart. The deep green velvet dress she wore fit tight against her skin. I wanted nothing more than to forget about the party and find out if she was wearing the black lace set I'd seen her in at the cabin underneath. But I was good. I kept my hands to myself even though I was itching to feel her again.

Lil stopped us at the door when we walked in. "You weren't supposed to bring a date!" she bites before turning to Charlie and sarcastically adding, "No offense, love. I'm sure you're a wonderful woman."

"Sorry, Lil. But I bet Tara and Smoke would get along great, and I know he didn't bring anyone tonight," I say gently, trying to defuse the situation and soothe my own anger at her comments about Charlie.

"I can go if I need to," Charlie offers with a sad smile on her face. "I mean, we just met a few hours ago and I didn't know you were involved."

Lilian holds up her hand and shouts, "He's not!" She clears her throat and quiets her voice, "I'm sorry. It's my fault. I tried to set him up with someone and I'm no matchmaker," she says with a hint of a laugh. "Stay, please. Enjoy the party! Just keep T-Rex here in line." She gives me a once-over, looks at Charlie, then gives me a wink. I shake my head, smiling at the quick change in her tone.

Everything inside is exactly the same as it was two weeks ago. Everything except the look on Tara's face: a mixture of sadness and jealousy. I'm okay with that. I place my hand on the small of Charlie's back and guide her to the food table. I'm not the least bit hungry, but I do need to drop off her cookies. I place them in the middle of the table, moving Marsha's centerpiece out of the way so that everyone can see them.

Just as I turn back to Charlie, the angelic-looking woman with bright blonde hair and ice-blue eyes steps up to us. She hands us both a Christmas Cracker from the wicker basket she carries and as she turns to walk away, she shoots a wink over her shoulder. *Damn. It was her.*

"What's this?" Charlie asks, turning the cracker over in her hands.

I smile, "That's a Christmas Cracker. You make a wish then crack it. There's always a little hat inside and a couple of toys. You're supposed to break one between two people and whoever gets the bigger side is the one whose wish comes true."

"Oh," she says, looking down at it. "Do you want to crack one with me?"

I give her mine, closing her hand around them both, "That's okay." Our eyes meet and I lower my head, speaking softly into her ear. "My wish has already come true."

Her cheeks turn pink and she pulls her bottom lip between her teeth. With a snap, she cracks the first one. The tiny toy falls onto the floor and I reach to pick it up. Miniature dog tags. I look around the room for the woman with the blonde hair but don't see her anywhere. Charlie pulls the hat out to find log cabins lining the edges. *Okay, not weird at all. Now I wish I'd kept mine just to see what was inside.*

When she cracks the second one, mine, she's careful not to let the toy drop. For the second time, I see that the toy is a miniature rolling pin. She lets out a small "aww" then gasps. I can't help myself but to pull the purple hat from the cracker before she can blink. Tiny, thumbprint cookies, like the ones I used to make with my grandma right down to the chocolate kisses in their middles, line the edges. My eyes go wide and I snap my head up to look at her.

"Want to make some lemon bars in the middle of nowhere with a tiny ninja?" she asks with a smile so bright it rivals the sun.

"Y-You remember?"

"I remember everything," she whispers.

She jumps in my arms, dropping the contents of both crackers on the floor, and kisses me deeply. I twist a hand into her hair, pulling her closer, begging her lips for entrance with the tip of my tongue. Everyone in the room disappears; it's just the two of us. Sliding my hand up her side, I reach one of her perfect peaks and palm it. She jerks back, breaking the kiss, and swats my hand.

"We are in public!" she quietly snaps.

The room is silent and all eyes are on us. A snicker escapes my lips. "Yes ma'am," I say, letting her feet touch the floor. She grabs my hand and drags me from the room, waving at Lil and Knox on the way out. "Nice to meet you!" she tosses Lil's way as she jogs by. The look of surprise on their faces tells me I'll have some explaining to do later. *You'll never believe what one wish can do.*

Grandma Jean's Thumbprint Cookies

Makes 36

Ingredients:

1 ¾ cups + 2 tablespoons all purpose flour
¾ teaspoon baking soda
1 pinch salt
½ cup softened butter
½ cup creamy peanut butter
½ cup, lightly packed, brown sugar
½ cup sifted powdered sugar
1 large egg, room temperature
1 teaspoon vanilla
36 unwrapped chocolate kisses (or substitute chocolate chips)

Directions:

1. Whisk together flour, baking soda, and salt in

a medium bowl and set aside.

2. In a stand mixer or separate medium bowl, cream butter, sugars and peanut butter until fluffy. (about 2-3 minutes) Add egg and vanilla, beat to combine. Slowly add dry ingredients and beat on low until just combined. Don't over beat! Cover the bowl and refrigerate for 1 hour.

3. Shape the dough into slightly smaller than golf-ball sized balls, roll them in sugar and place on a lined baking sheet about 2 inches apart. Press your thumb in the middle of the balls to make an indentation in the top of the cookie. Pop the cookies back in the refrigerator to chill while oven is pre-heating.

4. Pre-heat oven to 350F

5. Bake cookies for about 12 minutes. Immediately place chocolate kisses on the tops of each cookie. (Or re-indent tops and drop a few chocolate chips in the wells.) Let the cookies cool on the baking sheet for about 10 minutes.Then move them to a wire rack to cool completely.

Enjoy!

Battlefield Special Cocoa (Made at Home)

Serves Two

Ingredients:

¼ cup and a tablespoon of sugar
A pinch of salt
⅛ cup of unsweetened cocoa
¼ cup water hot
½ teaspoon vanilla extract
2 cups milk

Optional Extras:

Mini Marshmallows
Chocolate Syrup

But don't skip the peppermint stick!
1. Mix sugar, cocoa, and salt in a saucepan and add water. Over medium heat, bring to a boil,

stirring constantly for about two minutes until chocolate is smooth.

2. Add in milk and stir together until hot, but don't bring to a boil.

3. Take cocoa off heat and add vanilla.

4. Drop in marshmallows and add a peppermint stick!

Enjoy!

Acknowledgements

We made it to the end!! Thank YOU, kind reader, for coming on this journey with me! If you fell in love with Lieutenant Lumbersnack and the tiny ninja as much as I did, be on the lookout for a continuation of their story coming sometime in 2024.

To whom this novella was dedicated: KJ! Please never stop sending me your streams of consciousness. They turn into some of the best ideas for both of us! Write me all the fun stuff. I need A&L like, yesterday. Thank you for being a sounding board for all my crazy, for cheering me on constantly, and for being an all-around amazing bestie! Could *not* have done this without you!!! Giant hugs from miles and miles away! FaceTime dance party soon? Yes? Yes. I love you!!

Amandaaaaaa! Amanda Nichole, author of Unawakened Fate, Fate Awakened, Preso Destino (on Kindle Vella now!) and many more to come. My author bestie, the best of the best. Thank you for everything you do! Thanks for not telling me I was crazy and for simply stating, "Okay, you've got four weeks; go!" It's been a bit longer than four weeks, but we made it! Your eyes on Christmas and your feedback have been life! Wouldn't have made it this far without you, lovely! I love you!!

To Artemas J. R. Broyles (check out her books on Amazon), Ruby Spark (hers too!), Nook (where Lilian got her name and personality), Nessa (her debut releases December 21, 2023), N.J. Rodman (check out her book, Secrets and Songbirds), Raffy (who has been waiting for this since I wrote the first word), all the writers in Megen Mossgrove's early morning writing sprints (watch out for her debut, The Wingbreaker!), all the amazing folks associated with Between the Pages, and a host of people I'm sure I'm missing but it is currently 5:18AM and ya girl is tired! I love each and every one of you and am immensely grateful to know you!! Thank you all for pushing me when I felt like giving up!

To my Honey Bunches of Oats, who puts up with me, believes in me, does all he can to empower me, and supports me every step of the way through this thing we call life. I love you more than air. Thank you.

About the Author

Juliet is a wife, mom, and wearer of many hats. She hails from Memphis, TN and loves spending her time with her husband and two kids. And their plethora of animals ranging from dogs to chickens. You'll find her more often than not with her nose in a book. Or listening to an audiobook. If she isn't adulting or reading, she's writing. Writing has been her passion since she was young and she's incredibly excited to finally get to share her work with the world! She is a dreamer of dreams and a lover of love! And spice! ;) She is a wanderer, but she's never lost. Come wander with her!

A few of the places she wanders:
Facebook: Juliet Thomas - Author
Instagram: @justwanderingnotlost3
TikTok: @justwandering_notlost

If you haven't yet, check out my New Beginnings series! Books 1 and 2 are available on KU and in buyable ebook and print formats! Also, check out book 3, Uncertain, uploaded in episodic format on Kindle Vella! Just please be mindful of the trigger warnings!

Printed in the USA
CPSIA information can be obtained
at www.ICGtesting.com
JSHW021106241223
54127JS00003B/170